THE WITCH WHO FILLED IN THE PICTURE

PIXIE POINT BAY BOOK 3

EMMA BELMONT

EMMA ONLINE

Emma loves hearing from her readers!

You can contact her at the links below.

Website: emmabelmont.com

Newsletter: emmabelmont.com/newsletter

Thanks!

1

"Ms. Seaver," someone called, loud enough to be heard above the din.

Inklings New & Used Books, the large three-story store on the Towne Plaza, was positively packed. Maris turned and peered into the crowd, and saw Mikhail Galkin hurrying toward her, both hands outstretched.

"I am delighted you could make it," he said, with just a hint of an exotic Russian accent. He grasped both her hands and, cheek to cheek, gave her an air kiss on one side, and then the other. "Thank you so much for coming."

"I wouldn't have missed it for the world, Mr. Galkin," she told him. "It's not every day we have an international art exhibit in Pixie Point Bay."

Tall, with sandy brown hair and a goatee to match, Maris guessed that he was in his mid-forties. He was looking very smart this evening in his tailored blue blazer and lavender turtleneck.

"*Please*," he said, "call me Mikhail. When you say 'Mr. Galkin', I expect to turn around and see my father." Then he gave her a wry smile. "Although in truth, he was Comrade Galkin."

Maris laughed a little. "Very well, Mikhail. Then I must insist you call me Maris."

From the beginning of his stay at the B&B, the art dealer had been a bit formal. She'd chalked it up to cultural differences, or perhaps that she owned the B&B and attached lighthouse. But here, at his temporary art exhibit, he seemed very much in his element.

He dropped her hands, bowed his head, and clicked his heels. "Of course, Maris," he said grinning. "Now, may I show you the exhibit?"

"That would be wonderful," she said, smiling and inclining her head.

As they made their way among the many bookshelves and people, Maris was glad she'd spent a little extra time picking her wardrobe. Although it was evening, most of the attendees wore business casual attire, as did she. Her black silk skirt with its small white floral print fell well below the knee, and matched her ruffled white blouse with black trim at the cuffs. The patent black heels were stylish, but low enough to be comfortable for the standing and walking she was anticipating.

Maris recognized a number of the people who were mingling with their plastic cups of wine. Long-time residents and shopkeepers mixed with the usual compliment of tourists, but the upscale dress of several people carrying the exhibit catalog spoke to prospective buyers.

The bookstore's existing recessed lighting was bright and cheery, although Maris spotted extra spot lamps that had been brought in—some with colored film over their fronts. Interestingly they weren't necessarily pointed at the artwork, but highlighted different parts of the ceiling with washes of color.

Mikhail made his way to the edge of the room and the large easels that were lined up in front of the books.

"First," he said, "as you can see, this is a multi-artist show. Some of the talent is local, some from further afield. Many of the latter are old acquaintances whose work I like to display whenever I can. But one of my favorite painters is the Pixie Point Bay watercolorist Clio Hearst."

"Clio Hearst," Maris said, tilting her head. "I'm afraid I'm not familiar with her work."

"You are in the majority, but I would like to change that." Mikhail led her to a small grouping of almost photorealistic images. "I think you might be particularly interested in her work because of the subject matter." Smiling broadly, Mikhail turned back to Maris. "As you see, one of her favorite subjects might be familiar to you."

"Oh, my goodness," Maris exclaimed, "the lighthouse and B&B." The details in the attached two-story Victorian were positively lifelike. The many gables and traditional windows were accurate, as was the coloring.

The conical white tower topped with its glass optics house glowed against a stunningly vibrant sunset. "She's really managed to capture the...spirit of the place." Maris had to smile to herself, since the Old Girl actually did have a spirit. She regarded Mikhail. "They're absolutely beautiful. I can definitely see why she's one of your favorites."

Mikhail nodded. "A local artist who makes the most of the local environment." He gestured to the nearby paintings. "These are all part of her Coastside Series."

Maris stepped closer and peered at the images of the bay and the pier. Tide pools seemed to brim with life, and the Pixie Point Bridge dramatically spanned a canyon on the coast. But no matter the subject, tiny brush strokes in their hundreds, maybe even thousands, created a vivd impression that seemed to surpass real life.

"These are remarkable," she said.

"Please excuse us," someone said from behind.

Maris and Mikhail turned to see Minako and Alfred Page, the owners of the bookstore and hosts for the evening's gala. They were both holding platters of delicious looking *hors d'oeuvres.*

"May I offer you some warm salmon shu-mai," Minako said, pointing to it, "also vegetable spring rolls, butternut squash with gouda pot stickers, and hand rolls of spicy yellowtail sushi."

"You certainly may," Maris said, taking a small paper plate and napkin from the tray. "Minako, you've really outdone yourself."

The diminutive Asian store owner beamed at her, her sleek black hair swaying as she bobbed her head. "Thank you," she said. "We also have some liquid refreshments."

"Japanese whisky and sake," Alfred said, holding his tray forward. It was covered in little ceramic sake glasses of all shapes and colors, some with amber liquid, and some with clear. The heady scent of the alcohol mixed nicely with the aromatic smell of the warm food.

Mikhail selected a shot of whisky. "Thank you," he said, and lifted the little glass to both of them. "And thank you again for hosting the gala. You have done a magnificent job."

As one of the largest establishments in

Pixie Point Bay, Maris was hard-pressed to think of another place that could have hosted it. Certainly there was no other that could have done it with as much style.

"I'll try these scrumptious delights to begin with," she said as she chose the salmon shumai and the spicy yellowtail hand roll. Though she would have loved to take two of everything, her ongoing quest for lower cholesterol and weight loss stopped her. "Thank you."

"Truly," Alfred said smiling. "It's very much–"

"Our pleasure," Minako said.

Maris grinned at them as they resumed circulating among the guests. Though Alfred was of a medium height and build, he still towered over his petite wife. And with his blonde hair and bespectacled blue eyes, they couldn't have looked more different. But Maris couldn't think of another couple that she'd met that seemed so together.

As the warm salmon shumai melted in her mouth, she detected a hint of scallion and ginger. The combination was perfect.

"Good, is it not?" Mikhail said smiling. Maris could only nod, as she enjoyed the tender texture and just the right amount of soy sauce seasoning. "I think I ate a whole tray during the setup. Minako and Alfred made everything themselves."

Maris covered her mouth with the napkin. "Wow," she muttered. She was going to have to see if they'd be willing to share the recipe.

"If you can stand my company for just another minute," Mikhail said, "may I introduce you to Clio?"

"Mmm," Maris said, nodding after she swallowed. "I'd love to meet her."

He glanced around the room. "Ah, there she is."

Maris followed him to a slim woman who appeared to be in her early thirties. Her auburn hair had been gathered and pinned behind her head and her bright blue eyes gazed at them as they approached. She was holding a tiny sake cup, and chatting with a few people. But as Mikhail approached, she excused herself and came forward to meet them.

"Maris Seaver," Mikhail said to her, "I would like you to meet the artist who painted the lovely photos of your lighthouse." He inclined his head to her. "Clio Hearst."

Clio's eyes widened and she smiled as she thrust out her hand. "You own the lighthouse?" she asked.

"I do," Maris said, shaking her hand.

"I absolutely adore it. It's one of my favorite subjects."

Maris glanced back at the artwork. "So I saw. And I must say, you've really managed to capture the magic of the place."

"Oh thank you," Clio said, glancing downward. "I hope I did it justice. But it's wonderful to hear you approve."

"How could she not?" Mikhail said. "But if you two ladies will excuse me, I think I might see a prospective buyer." He gave them a quick bow and hurried off.

Maris turned to the artist. "Really, all of your work is amazing. Not just the lighthouse—even if it's my favorite. I can see why Mikhail chose to feature you."

A little color rose to Clio's cheeks. "That's so kind of you. I–"

The sound of raised voices interrupted her. Maris turned to see Aurora Puddlefoot arguing heatedly with a well-dressed man that she recognized. Like Mikhail, art critic Langston Spaulding and his wife were guests at the B&B and had come for the express purpose of the art gala. But at the moment the artsy couple were being assailed by the owner of the town's gift store, Magical Finds.

The older woman, dressed in her typical exotic attire, was gesticulating wildly. The long sleeves of her bright red robes fluttered, and her long platinum braids swayed to and fro. Her exaggerated makeup and bright red lipstick made it easy to see her facial expression, which was consternated anger. Even her violet cloth head wrap was tilting to one side.

"That despicable man," Clio said vehemently. "He has always belittled my work."

Now Maris realized that the art critic and Aurora were standing in front of one of Clio's paintings.

Langston was worked up as well, jabbing his finger nearly in Aurora's face. He was wearing a dapper black suit, black shirt and black tie, while his wife was wearing a deeply cut, burgundy evening dress. But as Maris watched in disbelief, he took off his designer glasses as though he was getting ready to fight.

"Good grief," Maris muttered. Certainly he wasn't actually going to have a physical altercation with Aurora. Although probably only in her late fifties, she was twenty years older than Langston and a foot shorter.

Maris had just been about to say something when Mikhail rushed to them and interposed himself. Although both parties managed to back up a pace, and their voices dropped a notch, they were still pointing at each other—until Mikhail's head jerked back and he grabbed his nose.

Everyone froze and there was stunned silence in the room.

"Oh my god," Clio whispered.

Blood was dripping down Mikhail's chin.

Alfred hurried to them and gently grasped Aurora's shoulders and led her away.

"That man is an idiot," Aurora declared, looking at the art critic over her shoulder. "An *idiot*."

Minako ran to Mikhail with a wad of napkins, which he took and put under his nose. At the same time Jayde Langston clutched her husband's arm and pulled him in the opposite direction. Gingerly holding his nose, Mikhail headed toward the men's room.

Clio frowned and shook her head. "Of all the people who would come here," she muttered under her breath. When Maris looked at her, she added, "He's called my work 'Thomas Kinkade meets Bob Ross' and 'a derivative mashup of derivative mashups'." Maris's eyebrows rose as she watched the Langstons disappear into the crowd. "That's how people like him make their living." Clio finished her sake in a single gulp. "By being pretentious and picking public fights." She looked at her empty cup. "I think I'll get another."

As she left, Minako and Alfred appeared in the center of the room, each smiling and holding a platter. "Please, everyone. We invite you to try–"

"Our famous spicy edamame," Alfred said. They moved in opposite directions toward the small clusters of guests. "It's a secret recipe–"

"Handed down in my family for three generations," Minako said, offering the tray to some guests, who smiled and took the little paper cups filled to the brim with the shelled soy beans.

Slowly, the murmur of conversation returned.

Maris glanced across the room and spied Jill Maxwell. When the nurse practitioner saw her, she smiled and waved. Maris waved back. As Jill turned to answer a woman who'd spoken to her, Maris watched as they both faced the painting behind them. The nurse was pointing to the old fashioned nurse's hat that the subject of the painting was wearing, and then she made a motion as if she were putting one on. The two women laughed, just before a group of other attendees obscured them from view.

As the gathering returned to normal, Maris drifted to one of the third floor's large front windows. To her pleasant surprise, she could just make out the revolving beam of the lighthouse in the distance. But then, to her shock, the beam winked at her. Maris nearly dropped her spicy yellowtail handroll. The Old Girl was signaling to her that trouble was brewing.

Not only did the Pixie Point Bay lighthouse have the best record of rescues in North America, it was a magical being named Claribel. Maris had no doubt that the later fact had helped to create the former. Although she had a special bond with the Old Girl—like her ancestors before her—she'd never seen her signal before. For a moment she could only stare, but the beam had already resumed its constant rotation.

As she considered for a moment, she thought back on the scuffle between Aurora, Langston, and Mikhail. That had to be it, and of course Claribel had known. Maris smiled at the rotating beam and whispered, "Thanks, Old Girl."

2

———

As Maris finished her delectable yellowtail handroll she decided it was time to freshen her lipstick—and get away from the *hors d'oeuvres*. Inside the women's room, Maris set her purse on the long counter in front of the mirror and took out her lipstick. But as she pulled off the cap, she realized someone else was at the far end of the mirror.

Strangely enough, she and Aurora Puddlefoot had never met. Though Maris had passed her gift shop often, she'd never taken the time to stop in. The shop owner was touching up her rather eccentric makeup, which now Maris could clearly see. Over her immaculate eyebrows were two graceful arches of tiny red dots that matched her brilliant lipstick. The effect was unusual and yet somehow not unpleasant. Maris picked up her purse and moved next to her.

"Good evening, Ms. Puddlefoot," she said. "My name is Maris Seaver."

"Aurora knows who you are," she said to her own reflection as she finished with the red dots, "and is pleased to meet you."

For a moment, Maris frowned and was tempted to look behind her. It was as though Aurora was speaking of someone else in the room.

The shopkeeper glanced sideways at her. "Aurora believes you are the owner of the lighthouse and B&B. Is she correct?"

"She is correct," Maris said, still trying to get her bearings. Was Aurora referring to herself in the third person?

"Ah yes," she said, turning back to the mirror with the lip gloss applicator. "The very same as in the paintings outside. Quite beautiful."

Maris turned to the mirror with her own lipstick. "I couldn't agree more, both in terms of the lighthouse and the paintings."

"Aurora is glad to hear it," she said, touching up her lipstick. "Clio Hearst is a supremely talented young lady." She cast a disdainful glance at the bathroom door. "No matter what that *idiot* says." She put away the lipstick and took out some blush. "Do you know that this fool was in Aurora's establishment today? Oh yes. She kicked him out after he asked if her makeup was inspired by Ronald McDonald or Bozo."

Maris had to stifle a laugh. Suddenly the door to the restroom swung open, and Jayde Spaulding rushed inside. Without looking to the right or left she hurried to the mirror and gave her hair a quick finger brush. Then she puckered her lips and frowned. She opened her purse and began to rummage through it, but froze when she realized she wasn't alone. Her eyebrows shot up when she saw Aurora, and she grabbed her purse and rushed out the door.

Aurora frowned. "Awkward," she said, and put away the blush. Without another word, she picked up her purse and exited.

As Maris finished her lipstick, she couldn't decide if Aurora was referring to the situation or Jayde, since awkward could have easily been used to describe both—and even Aurora herself.

Maris glanced at her watch. It was time to call it a night. Not only did the B&B usually have an early morning start, it would be good to avoid any more temptation from Minako's third generation recipes.

Outside again, she saw that the crowd had thinned a little, allowing better viewing of the artwork. As Mikhail had said, several artists and styles were represented. Two large portraits sat side by side but from their strange cubist shapes, Maris couldn't tell if they were men or women. There was a still life of citrus fruit in a metal bowl, followed by an almost completely white canvas with only a small rectangle of blue in its center. It was an eclectic mix, but the featured artist was clearly Clio. She stood in front of her artwork and in the center of a small group of admirers. True to her word, she had a new cup of sake, and was smiling and laughing as she posed for photos with various people.

After the altercation between the art critic and Aurora, Maris was glad to see that the evening was ending on a positive note for her.

She crossed to Minako and Alfred, who were still circulating with trays of food and drink. "What a delightful evening this has been," she told them. "Your shop is beautiful, the food was extraordinary, and you are wonderful hosts.

"Thank you," Minako answered, beaming. "This is high praise indeed–"

"From the owner of the best B&B on this coast or any other," Alfred told her.

Maris smiled. "Thank you." She eyed the paintings and onlookers. "Judging by the number of attendees, it seems you and Mikhail have had a huge success."

"We truly hope so," Alfred said.

"For Mikhail's sake," Minako added.

Maris nodded, and turned to see if she could spot Mikhail anywhere, but suddenly there was shouting coming from the ground floor, followed by a wild shriek.

3

Alarmed guests stopped what they were doing. Minako and Alfred were the first ones to recover, setting down their trays and heading for the stairs. Only then did Maris understand what Claribel had meant. The Old Girl had been warning her of *more* trouble, not the altercation. She hurried after the bookstore owners.

"There's a dead body!" someone screamed.

In another few moments they'd arrived at the ground floor. One of the guests that Maris didn't recognize was frantically waving at a door in the back of the store.

"Outside," he said. "Hurry! This way!"

Maris, Minako, and Alfred ran after him

to an elevated loading dock in the back alley. Large wooden crates crowded the area, but at the edge, not twenty feet from them, lay a body. The three of them rushed over. Minako let out a small squeal.

"Stay back," Alfred said, holding out his arm. "Don't look." Minako instantly turned away.

But even from where she stood Maris could see that it was Langston Spaulding. He was sprawled on his back, his lifeless eyes staring up at the sky. Maris felt her stomach sink and swallowed hard. There was a knife sticking out of his chest, and a glistening patch of wetness stained the black shirt around it. Under the harsh glare of the dock's fluorescent lights, the art critic's unmoving face seemed slightly green. Maris put a hand to her mouth.

Alfred stepped over the dead man's legs to his other side.

"I just came out for a smoke," the guest said. He was still clutching the cigarette in a trembling hand. "Oh, dear God, I almost fell right on top of him. It's the art critic, isn't it? The one who was arguing with the gypsy."

Alfred crouched and checked for a pulse

at the side of Langston's neck. When he straightened up, he shook his head. "Minako, I think we should–"

"Call the police," she said, and hurried back inside.

4

At the sound of the siren and the sight of the revolving red lights, all eyes turned to the storefront. Most of the guests who remained had elected to wait on the upper floors. But as Sheriff Daniel "Mac" McKenna came through the front door, Alfred and Minako were waiting for him, while Maris sat in the nearest reading area.

"Sheriff," Alfred said, coming forward and extending his hand. "Alfred Page." He indicated Minako. "And my wife, Minako. We're the owners of Inklings."

As they shook hands, Mac said, "I understand it was Minako who called the emergency line and that there's been a murder."

"Yes, I'm afraid so," Minako said, and Maris noticed that she looked a bit more pale than usual. "Maris was with us when we found the body."

"Maris?" Mac said. She got up from the low chair and came forward as the sheriff turned to her. "Maris," the sheriff said, smiling at her. "I didn't realize you'd be here."

She returned his warm smile. "The Pages were putting on an art exhibit, and I'm one of the guests." She looked up the stairs at some of the faces watching them. "Among many others."

Mac followed her gaze. "I see."

"Some of the guests have already gone," Alfred said, taking his wife's hand. "They were–"

"Anxious to leave," Minako said.

Mac studied them both for a moment. "Do you have a list of the invitees?"

Alfred nodded. "Yes. Mikhail provided it to us so we could plan."

"And we also have a guest book," Minako added. She indicated the open ledger on the wine table.

Maris noticed a slight tremble in their

clasped hands and realized they must have been on their feet all day getting the store and food ready. Mac must have noticed something as well. "Why don't you folks have a seat," he said, indicating the area where Maris had been waiting. "Please."

Alfred led Minako that way, and they both quickly sat, still holding hands. Mac watched them, and then eyed Maris. "You were there when the body was found?"

"Not initially," she said. "One of the other guests had gone out to the loading dock for a cigarette."

"Is he still here?"

Maris pointed to the man pacing near the cash register. When he saw her pointing, he abruptly stopped. Mac glanced back at the Pages, then lowered his voice as he leaned in toward Maris.

"How are you doing?" he asked.

Maris smiled a little. Though she'd been as shocked as the rest of them at the discovery of the body, she'd managed to recover much more quickly. Whether it had been Claribel's warning, or the fact that she'd never met the art critic, or maybe even that she was getting used to bodies turning up in Pixie Point Bay, she didn't know. But she was definitely doing better than either the Pages or the man with the cigarette.

"I'm doing fine, actually," she said. "Do you want to see the loading dock?"

Mac nodded. "That's exactly what I want to see."

"All right," she said. "Let me just get them some water."

Maris quickly headed to the wine and water table near the entrance and snatched up three bottles. The first two she took to Alfred and Minako. "Drink," she told them. Though they smiled weakly as they accepted the bottles, they made no move to open them. "Stay hydrated," she told them. "This is just the beginning."

As one, they blinked at her, and then looked at each other. They both twisted off the caps and took long drinks.

Satisfied, Maris headed back to Mac. "This way," she said. As they approached the man with the cigarette, Maris held out a bottle of water to him. "Please have some water, Mr. ..."

"Temple," he said taking the bottle. "Lewis Temple." He looked directly at Mac. "I didn't do it."

Mac took the notepad from his breast pocket. "No one said you did, Mr. Temple." He made a quick note. "But I'd like to ask you to remain here for just a few more minutes." He closed the notepad. "Can you do that?"

The man looked between the bottle of water in one hand, and the cigarette in the other, as though he were trying to decide between them. "Can I smoke out front?"

"Yes," Mac said, nodding toward the entrance. "I'll find you there."

In the back, on the loading dock, Langston Spaulding's body was right where they'd left it. The dock's bright overhead lights cast harsh shadows making the entire area seem a little ghoulish.

Mac went to the body and crouched down. He squatted there for several seconds, peering intently at the knife protruding from Spaulding's chest. When he stood, he made a few notes.

"So Mr. Temple stumbled across the body when he came out here to smoke," he said.

"Right," Maris said. "Alfred, Minako, and I were on the third floor when we heard him screaming." She looked back to the dock's door. "We ran out here and saw immediately it was Langston Spaulding."

"You know the victim?" Mac asked, looking up at her.

Maris shook her head. "Not as such. He's an art critic, here for the exhibit. He and his wife are staying at the B&B."

"His wife?" Mac asked, taking notes.

"Jayde," Maris answered.

Mac nodded. "And who is this Mikhail who gave a guest list to the Pages?"

"That would be another guest at the B&B, Mikhail Galkin. He's the organizer of the event, and an art dealer."

Mac looked around at the crowded dock, full of wooden crates in all shapes and sizes. "So this art dealer is using Inklings to host an exhibit." Maris nodded. "He invites you, guests from the town, and anyone else who will come, including art critic Langston Spaulding and his wife, Jayde."

"Yes," Maris said.

"So everyone is here, having wine and

cheese, when suddenly Mr. Temple says there's been a murder."

Maris narrowed her eyes. "Not quite."

"Ah," Mac said, pencil poised above notepad.

Maris grimaced a bit. "Langston and Aurora Puddlefoot had an argument, about the work of Clio Hearst, a local artist that Mikhail is representing."

Mac jotted down the names and, without looking up said, "The owner of Magical Finds?"

"Yes," Maris said. "I ran into her in the ladies room. She'd tossed Langston out of her store earlier today." Mac raised his eyebrows. "Then, this evening, when he'd disparaged Clio's work, Aurora had quarreled with him."

"There were raised voices and words were said?" he asked.

Maris shook her head again. "I'm afraid it was a little more than that." Mac closed the notebook. "Mikhail tried to come between them, between Aurora and Langston." She glanced at the body. "And he somehow took a blow to the face, which gave him a bloody nose."

Mac scowled. "Someone punched him?"

"Oh no," Maris said quickly. "That's not at all how it looked. I think it was an accident."

Mac considered for a moment. "All right," he finally said. "I think it's time to speak with Aurora, Jayde, and Mikhail."

"I wonder if we could speak to Jayde first," Maris suggested. "So that she can leave."

Mac nodded. "I don't see why not." He turned to go.

Maris looked at the body one last time. "Maybe the knife will have fingerprints."

Mac paused and pursed his lips for a moment, following her gaze. "It's possible, but it's not a knife."

Maris blinked at him. "It's not?"

He motioned her over to where he stood. "It has some sort of blade," he said pointing at it. "But look at the handle. The metal shaft is bent at an angle, a perfect ninety degrees, twice."

Maris had to look at it before she realized what he was saying. The metal shaft was some type of rod that took an almost zigzag path. It had a round wooden handle as well, also not very knife-like.

"It's some type of tool," he said. He looked

around the dock. "Maybe something used out here."

At that moment, the door to the loading dock opened and Alfred appeared. "The coroner has arrived."

5

———

Maris waited with the Pages as Mac filled the coroner in on the details near the front of the store. They sat where she had left them, still holding their water bottles.

"How are you two holding up?" she said, sitting down with them.

Minako shook her head, staring at the ground. "He complimented the potstickers," she whispered, then looked up at Maris. "Only one hour ago."

"I'm afraid it's a bit of a shock," Alfred said, patting his wife's knee.

Maris sighed. "I know what you mean."

"Oh, of course you do," Alfred said. "You were at the credit union when the manager died."

"Awful business," Minako said. Then she regarded Maris. "How did you cope?"

Maris smiled at her. "At first, I drank some water and took a seat." She thought back to that day. "Directly after, I tried to be useful to the police. In the days that followed, I tried to stay busy."

"Thank you," Minako said.

"Good advice," Alfred said.

They looked at each other. "I'll go get the list of attendees invited," he said.

"I'll go get the guest book," Minako answered.

At that point, the coroner proceeded to the loading dock and Mac went outside. He spoke briefly with a furiously puffing Lewis Temple, who then left. By the time he returned, the forensics team had also arrived.

"The body and the coroner are on the loading dock in the back," he said, pointing to the door in the back of the store.

Alfred and Minako both returned and handed over the invitation list and the guestbook.

"Thank you," the sheriff said. "There's no need to detain most of the guests. I'll be speaking with Jayde Spaulding, Aurora Puddlefoot, and Mikhail Galkin."

The couple looked a little relieved. "We'll let everyone know," Alfred said.

"But Aurora left some time ago," Minako added.

Maris stood and joined them, and they all moved to the stairs. The Pages were definitely looking better, and hopefully feeling better as well.

Alfred said, "I think Jayde is on the second floor." He glanced up the stairs. "We'll start on the third floor and let the guests know it's okay to leave."

"If we see Mikhail," his wife said, "we'll let him know you want to speak with him."

Maris and Mac did indeed find Jayde on the next floor, in one of the bookstore's many sitting areas, and Maris was relieved to see Jill Maxwell sitting with her, holding her hand.

Jayde sat in a straight-backed chair, ghostly white, not moving. Even as Mac and Maris approached, she seemed not to see them. Jill smiled sympathetically at them.

Mac cleared his throat. "Mrs. Spaulding?"

When she didn't move, he exchanged a look with Maris and then with Jill. The nurse squeezed her hand. "Jayde, honey, it's Sheriff McKenna."

"Mrs. Spaulding," Mac said, his voice soft. "Are you possibly up to answering a few questions?"

Someone had draped a wool shawl over her shoulders, an odd juxtaposition with her dramatic dress. She blinked slowly and finally turned to Jill.

"The sheriff is here," the nurse said.

Mac crouched down in front of the poor woman. "We can certainly wait until later, Mrs. Spaulding."

Finally she seemed to see him. She took in the uniform and seemed to focus on the gold star badge. Then she looked into his face. "No," she said, her voice barely a whisper. "Let's do it now."

"Are you sure?" Jill asked. "Maybe–"

"If there's even the slightest chance that I can help," Jayde said, her voice gaining strength. "The sooner, the better."

Mac nodded. "I appreciate it, Mrs. Spaulding. That's exactly my reasoning." He glanced at Maris. "I understand you're staying at the B&B."

Jayde nodded. "We are, yes." Her face

screwed up and she covered her eyes with her palms. "I mean, I am." Slowly she lowered her hands to her lap, but Jill offered her a tissue and she used it to dab her eyes. "I'm sorry," she said, her voice trembling.

"Apparently there was an argument this evening," Mac said quietly. "Did you witness it?"

"Oh," Jayde said, rolling her eyes. "That bizarre woman. The one who owns the store. Have you questioned her?"

"Not yet," Mac said. "What did they argue about?"

She sniffed and shook her head. "The same thing he always argues about." She looked from Jill to Maris, and then back to Mac. "Art."

"And they disagreed?" Mac prompted.

Jayde put the tissue to her nose. "That was his job. To disagree. If an artist was getting any kind of notoriety, he took the opposite view."

"And I assume that Ms. Puddlefoot was upset by that," Mac said.

"She tried to punch him," Jayde declared. "Everyone saw it. Mikhail got between them, and she punched him instead."

"Did he have an argument with anyone else tonight?" Mac asked.

"Oh, he'd make snide comments," she said, shrugging. "But no one else took exception that I saw." She stared into her lap for a moment, and her lower lip began to tremble. "He was a wonderful husband," she said. "I know what people thought of him, but that was his public persona." She covered her face with her hands again. "God, what am I going to do?"

The metal rattling of the rolling gurney came from the first floor. Jayde shot to her feet and looked in that direction, causing Mac and Jill to stand as well. For a moment the woman swayed, but they steadied her.

"Are they taking him?" she gasped. She looked wildly from Maris to Jill and then Mac. "I have to go." She looked around for something. "I have to go with him."

Maris saw her purse on the floor next to the chair and picked it up. "That may not be a good idea," she said gently, as she handed the purse over.

"But–" Jayde sputtered, clearly panicked.

"I'm afraid you won't be permitted to ride in the coroner's van," Mac said.

"I don't care," she nearly shrieked. "I don't care. I'm going with him."

Jill put a hand on her arm. "The sheriff is right." She glanced at him. "But I'll give you a ride."

The woman was trembling now, but nodded repeatedly. "Yes. I'd appreciate that. I'd *so* appreciate that, Jill." She looked toward the stairs. "I...I just don't want him to be...alone."

Maris felt a lump in her throat, and Jill grimaced a little but nodded. "I understand."

"The B&B's front door will be open," Maris said quietly to the nurse. "Just knock on my door, first floor, end of the hall, if you need anything."

6

As Maris and Mac watched Jill help Jayde down the stairs, the sheriff turned to her. "You'll need to point out Mikhail Galkin and Clio Hearst to me, if they're still here."

After a quick search of the second floor, Maris led Mac up to the third floor. As expected, most of the guests had gone. But as Maris had guessed, the Pages were still cleaning up. Alfred pointed toward the area where most of the easels were located. Mikhail was with someone who looked like a buyer.

As they got closer, Maris said, "Here he is."

Both the art dealer and his prospective client saw them approaching. Mikhail quickly shook hands with the man. "I will call you tomorrow to finalize."

The customer only nodded, glanced at Mac, and hurried away.

Mikhail smiled at them, his nose swollen and red. "I assumed that you did not need to speak with the customers." His voice was a bit nasally, as if he had a cold.

"Correct," Mac said. "Mikhail Galkin?"

"At your service," he said, with a quick bow of his head and a click of his heels.

"Sheriff McKenna." Mac pointedly looked at Mikhail's nose. "Who punched you?"

The art dealer's eyebrows shot up. "No one." Then he gingerly touched his nose. "This was an accident. Hands and fingers were flying everywhere. As they say in the old country, I made the mistake of coming between the hammer and the anvil."

"So no idea?" Mac asked.

Mikhail shook his head. "It would please me to no end to say that it was Spaulding, God rest his soul, but I really do not know."

Mac took out his note pad. "And why would you like to say it was Spaulding?"

Mikhail smiled. "I would wear it as a badge of honor." But when Mac made a note,

Mikhail's smile slipped. "I have known Langston Spaulding for over twenty years. The man was as tasteless as he was vulgar. He was being purposely provocative regarding the work of Clio Hearst. In fact, there was no artist too big or successful—and I have known a few—who he did not deride with his particular brand of inflammatory rhetoric. "

"You were not an admirer," Mac concluded.

"He had none," Mikhail said, as though it was obvious.

Except for Jayde, Maris thought.

"Where were you when he was killed?" Mac asked.

He smiled at the sheriff. "I am pleased to say that I was with a number of different buyers—and I mean pleased for the sake of my clients, particularly Clio."

"Is she still here?" Maris asked.

The art dealer shook his head. "She found the whole thing very distressing when she learned of Spaulding's death. I believe she has gone home."

Mac looked up from his notes. "I'll need the names of the buyers you mentioned."

"Of course," Mikhail said. "I will be happy to provide them to you."

Mac nodded and closed his notepad. "That'll be it for tonight," he said. "But I'd like you to stay in town."

Mikhail paused for a moment and then looked at Maris. "I would be delighted to spend more time in this charming town, but I am not sure of my accommodations."

Maris smiled at them both. "I'm happy to say that the B&B would be delighted to extend your stay."

"Fine," Mac said. "I'll have to speak with Ms. Puddlefoot and Ms. Hearst tomorrow." He nodded to them both. "Thank you for your time."

7

In the morning, Maris headed down the B&B's hallway to the kitchen. If she hadn't known the way, she could simply have closed her eyes and followed her nose. The delicious smells of breakfast that wafted through the air were the culinary world's equivalent of a siren's call.

At the kitchen door, she didn't pause for an instant. "Good morning," she said, with her usual cheer. "What smells so incredible?"

As usual, Cookie was at the stove and looked over her shoulder smiling. "One of my specialties—and good morning."

It seemed that no matter how early Maris got up, Cookie was in the kitchen before her. Nor did Maris ever hear the diminutive chef, even though their rooms were close. She was as quiet and dependable as the daily fog.

In her early seventies, Ruth "Cookie" Calderon had been with Maris's Aunt Glenda for decades. The two of them had established a now time-honored routine, which Maris had quickly adopted: she took care of the evening wine and cheese, while Cookie prepared the breakfast buffet. The guests were on their own for lunch and dinner.

Maris looked over Cookie's shoulder. *"Breakfast Pie in a Skillet,"* she said, her mouth already watering. "My favorite."

Cookie nodded, her graying pony tail bobbing. She wore a short-sleeved cotton dress with a large floral print, though it was mostly covered with her apron.

In one of the big iron skillets that Cookie favored were layers of eggs, cheese, mushrooms, onions, and peppers. It was a delicious combination of textures and flavors that brought out the best in the ingredients. On occasion the B&B hosted returning guests who sometimes requested it.

Maris went to the lighted double oven and saw red-skinned potatoes roasting on cookie sheets with a light dusting of sea salt.

On the nearby counter were fresh strawberries and Cookie's oversized blueberry muffins.

"I guess I'll squeeze the orange juice," Maris said.

"That would be wonderful," Cookie replied.

As with the rest of the kitchen, the Victorian look was only a veneer. The large period butcher block, matching wooden stools, and the lace curtains gave the big room a period feel. But underneath it all was professional equipment, from the extra large microwave and immense brushed steel refrigerator to the generous double sinks and double oven. Maris brought out the state-of-the-art juicer and began to peel the oranges and drop the segments inside.

"How was the art gala last night?" Cookie asked, as she began moving the roasted potatoes to a warming tray.

Although a cardinal rule of the hospitality trade was to never stop working when you talked, Maris did just that as she turned to the chef. "Langston Spaulding was murdered."

Cookie stopped as well, her eyes wide as

she gaped at Maris. "Our guest?" She glanced upward and back to Maris. "*Murdered?*"

Maris nodded. "I'm afraid so."

"By who?"

Maris put a few more segments of orange into the juicer. "That's the question."

"Well you'd better have more details than that for me," Cookie said, as she moved the rest of the potatoes over.

Maris recounted the entire evening, including the argument with Aurora Puddlefoot.

"A hot-tempered one, Aurora," Cookie said, as she sliced the Breakfast Pie.

"To say the least," Maris said, pouring the fresh juice into a beautiful glass decanter. "Poor Mikhail got a bloody nose out of that little altercation."

Again Cookie stopped. "One of our guests was injured?"

Maris nodded. "I don't think it was bad though." She picked up the juice. "The one I'm worried about is Jayde."

Cookie put a hand to her chest for a moment. "The poor thing." She shook her head. Then her eyes went to the ceiling. "I did hear a car on the gravel late last night. Was that her?"

"I imagine so," Maris said, heading to the dining room. "Jill Maxwell was kind enough to give her a ride." She looked at the full warming trays. "Be right back for those."

After a few trips, the entire breakfast buffet was ready, including fresh coffee and hot water on tap. Maris took a moment and poured herself a nice cup of steaming java.

Back in the kitchen, Cookie was steeping some tea. "I hope Jayde is resting," the chef said. "I'll set aside a plate for her, for later."

"That'd be lovely, Cookie. Thank you."

A tiny, tinny harmonica-like meow drew their attention to the kitchen floor.

"Good morning, Mojo," Maris said.

The slightly pudgy and very fluffy little black cat looked up at her. Maris's Aunt Glenda, a blues music fan, had named him after George "Mojo" Buford, the harmonica player for legendary musician Muddy Waters. As his big orange eyes fixed on her, he meowed again, sounding exactly like a miniature version of the instrument.

"Breakfast time?" Maris asked. This time

he closed his eyes as he meowed. She reached down and smoothed her hand gently over the soft fur between his ears. "Gotcha."

Mojo lightly bounced over to his bowl as Maris went to the refrigerator. Inside she found the plastic container dedicated to his meals and opened it. The smell of smoked salmon wafted out, making Maris's stomach rumble.

"They say seafood increases the IQ," Cookie said, and sipped her tea. "At this point, Mojo must be a genius."

As the little cat waited patiently by his bowl, Maris filled it with salmon. "Is that true, Mojo?" In answer, he almost dove face first into the waiting fish, devouring it in great gulps. "Uh, yes." Maris laughed a little. "I see."

"Shall we?" Cookie asked, gesturing to the door.

This was a hospitality technique to which Maris had warmed immediately. Rather than hide in the kitchen for their meals, Cookie insisted they eat with the guests. It encouraged relaxed conversation all around, even between the guests themselves.

Maris served herself a not-too-large

helping of the Breakfast Pie, a few strawberries, and decided to skip the blueberry muffins. Just as she was sitting down across from Cookie, the Schellings came down.

"Good morning," Maris said, smiling at the young Swiss couple.

Andrin and Mia Schelling appeared to be in their mid-thirties. He was at least six feet tall and slim, with brunette hair and dark eyes, while she was nearly the opposite: short, blonde, blue-eyed, and a little chunky.

"Good morning," Andrin said, with an almost German-sounding accent. He grinned at the buffet and wasted no time in heading directly for it.

"Good morning," Mia said, pausing for a moment as she took in the room and the bay window. "Another beautiful foggy morning here in Pixie Point Bay."

"As always," Cookie said. "And then at mid-morning, it lifts. As always."

Mia smiled. "It's remarkable. And the lighthouse itself." She glanced behind her. "The most picturesque we've ever seen."

"And we've seen a few," Andrin said, bringing over a plate that was piled high.

"Is that right?" Maris said, then paused as

she considered for a moment. "But not in Switzerland." The country was land locked.

"Exactly," Andrin said, as Mia went to the buffet. "You might say this is a hobby of ours."

"Visiting lighthouses?" Cookie asked as she used the side of her fork to cut her slice of pie.

"Exactly," he said again. "On our vacations." He took a bite of the Breakfast Pie, made an appreciative sound, and gave Cookie the thumbs up sign. She smiled and nodded back.

"And what is it that you do when you're home?" Maris asked.

"Andrin is an investment banker," Mia said, "and I'm a digital artist. We live in Zurich."

Maris had, of course, been to their home town. In her twenty-five years of globetrotting from one hotel to another, she'd been to every major city in the world.

"Oh I adored that wonderful monastery in Einsedeln," she said.

Andrin quickly swallowed. "You know it?" he exclaimed. "Kloster Einsedeln?"

"Beautiful," Maris said, picking up a

strawberry. "The Gregorian chanting was ethereal."

For a few minutes the young couple chatted about the wonders in their part of the world, but eventually the conversation came back to Pixie Point Bay.

"We like to take photos of the lighthouses we visit," Andrin said, peeling the top off of his blueberry muffin and slathering the underside with butter. "In your opinion, where will we get the best view."

"I like to use them in my artwork," Mia added.

"Without a doubt," Maris said, "the best view is from the water."

"Oh!" Andrin said. "I would never have guessed."

"You capture not only the lighthouse and the bay," Maris said, "but the rocky coastline, the rolling hills above it, and the mountains to the east."

He exchanged an excited look with Mia. "Perfect."

"We have kayaks at the dock below," Maris said, "if you're in a sporting mood. But you can also charter a boat at the pier."

"Hmm," Mia said, considering. "From the kayak, we'd be pretty close to the water...."

"Maybe too close," Andrin said, "too much water in the foreground..."

"Let's go to the pier," Mia said.

They smiled at one another and Andrin said, "It's settled then." He got up and returned to the buffet for another plate. "This dish is wonderful, Cookie. What is it called?"

"Breakfast Pie in a Skillet," the chef said. "A specialty of the B&B."

"Breakfast Pie in a Skillet," he repeated, serving himself another slice. But when he returned to the table, he looked out the window at the fog. "Mia, maybe we can eat on the back porch and watch the lighthouse beam. What do you think?"

"Wonderful idea," she said, getting up and taking her plate. She smiled at Maris and Cookie. "It's not often we get this kind of opportunity. I hope you don't mind."

"Not at all," Maris said. "The beam up close in the fog is not to be missed. It almost seems to shimmer."

Mia and Andrin exchanged a quick look. "Let's go," he said.

As the Schellings headed toward the back of the house, Maris was surprised to see Jayde appear at the dining room door.

8

───────

"Jayde," Maris said, standing. The poor woman looked like hell. Black circles underlined her puffy red eyes, and her hair was in total disarray. Though she'd changed into a pair of slacks and a t-shirt, she hadn't bothered to put on shoes. She clutched a wad of tissues in one hand. "I didn't expect you down this early."

"I couldn't stay alone in my room any more," she said, her voice raspy and thin, "and I don't seem to be able to stop crying."

"Oh, Jayde," Maris said, going to her and helping her to a seat. "Of course you're going to cry. It's only natural."

"I didn't sleep," she said. "I can't get the image of him at the morgue out of my mind." Maris exchanged a look with Cookie, who got up and went to the kitchen. Tears pooled up in Jayde's eyes. "I...I wish I hadn't gone."

Maris took her hand. "Here's what you can do," she said. "Instead of dwelling on that image, search your memory for a happy one." When Jayde didn't respond, Maris squeezed her hand. "Can you think of a happy time with Langston? Did you ever laugh together at something?"

Jayde shook her head a little. "I...I don't know. I can't seem to remember anything."

"Maybe a time when you were in the car together, or at home, or maybe at a movie, or–"

"Oh," she said, perking up. "We were at the movies and he was bringing popcorn." She smiled a little. "But just as he sat down, the bucket tipped over—into my lap. You should have seen the look on his face." She laughed a little. "I told him to leave it there. That was my half." She dabbed at her eyes.

"And now," Maris said gently, "hold that thought. When another one comes up, if it's unpleasant in any way, remember that popcorn bucket. Pull that memory up instantly." She patted Jayde's hand. "I guarantee it'll work."

Just then Cookie returned with a cup of tea, and a plate that held two pieces of toast with butter and honey.

"Have a sip of tea," the chef said, sitting the cup in front of Jayde. "It's a special brew of mine."

Maris had to smile to herself. Not only was Cookie an amazing chef, her magical gift was for making potions. No matter what ailed you, Cookie's tea could help.

"You need to stay hydrated, Jayde," Maris said. "And I must say, it smells wonderful."

Jayde gingerly took the china teacup's handle, and took a little sip. Her eyebrows went up, and she took another. "It tastes wonderful," she whispered, and cleared her throat. She took yet another sip. "Mmm. Yes, that really helps."

Maris sighed with a bit of relief, and gave Cookie a grateful look before the chef returned to the kitchen. Some of Jayde's color was returning, and she glanced at the toast. Maris pushed the plate a bit closer.

"I'm going to get some strawberries," she said, standing up. She hoped that if she ate, it would encourage Jayde. "Can I get you some? Or maybe a slice of Breakfast Pie?"

Jayde shook her head. "I'm really not that hungry," she glanced at the toast again. "But maybe just a bite of toast."

By the time Maris sat down with her, Jayde had finished the first piece, and Maris had to smile. You could always trust Cookie and her teas. But as Jayde reached for the second piece she stopped, and her face screwed up.

"What is it?" Maris asked.

"An autopsy," Jayde whispered. "The coroner said there would have to be one."

Maris nodded and gave her a sympathetic look. "Yes, that would be standard. The same was required for my aunt." Jayde looked up at her. "The sheriff will be in touch with the results. Hopefully soon."

"Your aunt?" Jayde asked.

Maris told her the story of the suspicious fire and her aunt's heart attack. "It's why I came back to Pixie Point Bay," Maris said, with a little smile, "and then I never left."

At that moment, they both heard footsteps on the stairs and Mikhail appeared in the doorway. Though he'd been headed toward the buffet, he stopped in mid-stride when he saw Jayde. Though his nose was no longer red, it still appeared to be a bit swollen. He came directly to her and offered his hand. When she took it, he bowed his head a little.

"Please accept my sincere condolences," he said.

"Thank you," she said.

When he straightened, there was an awkward moment as neither of them seemed to want to look at each other. Finally Mikhail took a step back and said, "In the old country we have a saying. You cannot hide an awl in a sack." He smiled a little at Maris's quizzical look and then at Jayde. "It is no secret that your husband and I had our disagreements. My job is to promote art, and his was to critique it. It naturally brought us into conflict." He shrugged his shoulders. "But that is all. I never bore him ill will."

"I know," was all Jayde said.

Seemingly satisfied, Mikhail went to the buffet and when he returned, Maris was surprised to see that he'd brought a plate for Jayde.

"Please," he said, taking a seat. "It would do me good to see you take a bite." She seemed about to protest, but he added. "Just one and I will trouble you no further."

"Cookie's Breakfast Pie in a Skillet is my absolute favorite," Maris said, smiling as she stood. She set the chair back in place. "It's one of the reasons I've had to learn to push myself away from the table."

She took her plate to the door but waited just long enough to see Jayde take a bite of the Breakfast Pie. As she left the room, she nodded to herself. That had been good of Mikhail. Though she would have liked nothing better than to have peppered him with questions about the evening and his relationship with Langston, she wouldn't do that in front of Jayde.

In the kitchen, Cookie was already loading the dishwasher, and Maris helped her. As Cookie rinsed, Maris loaded. "I was thinking of visiting Magical Finds today," Maris said, matter-of-factly.

"Were you?" Cookie said, in a matching tone. "Shopping for something in particular?"

"No, not really," Maris said, taking a bowl from her and putting it in the bottom rack. "Just some window shopping."

"Uh huh," Cookie said, passing her a plate. "Maybe you'll run into Aurora Puddlefoot."

"Maybe," Maris said, smiling a little, "maybe."

Cookie dried her hands on a dish towel. "Well then, while you're out, would you pick up some sandwiches for lunch?"

"Of course," Maris said, closing the dishwasher and accepting the towel from Cookie. "What did you have in mind?"

"An assortment," the chef said. "I doubt that Jayde will feel like going out, and Bear will be stopping by later to help me with some landscaping."

"An assortment sounds great," Maris agreed. Adding sandwiches for Bear pretty much doubled the order. Their burly handyman had an appetite that matched his outsized proportions. "I'll pick them up on my way home."

9

Maris was lucky enough to find a parking spot directly in front of Magical Finds, an enormous building—and former inn—that occupied a corner lot on the Towne Plaza. Three stories tall, it was painted a pretty sky blue and trimmed in white around its many tall bay windows. Vintage signage in dark green and gold hung on both sides of the front double doors. As Maris opened one, a small bell attached to a spring at the top of it chimed.

Inside, Maris had to pause. The interior matched the impressive exterior.

"Wow," she muttered.

The expansive first floor must have once been an immense lobby. As far as the eye could see, it was stocked with all manner of merchandise being perused by a number of shoppers. She wandered over to the racks of postcards that stood to one side. One entire carousel was devoted to antique pictures of men and women in Victorian dress strolling past the town's various establishments. Several showed women in ornate hats and dresses posing in front of the gift store when it was an inn.

On the wall behind the postcards Maris was delighted to see some examples of Clio Hearst's work. One of them even featured Claribel. Next to the paintings were maps of the area, and a small antique bookcase with volumes about Pixie Point Bay and the environs. A particularly pretty binding caught Maris's eye: *The Magic of Pixie Point Bay.*

"Hmm," she murmured, picking it up. She turned to the introduction.

A WALK along the rocky shore of Pixie Point Bay is unlike any other. Otters frolic among the waves, some floating on their backs and beating the oysters on their stomachs with small rocks to get at the tender meat. A misty blow of air signals the presence of a dolphin...

WITH JUST A TINGE OF DISAPPOINTMENT, she replaced the book on the shelf. For a fraction of a second, she thought she'd read about the magic folk.

But then *Bustles and Parasols, the Clothing and Accoutrements of the American Woman* got her attention. This book, Maris noted, was filled with fine color illustrations of various types of feminine attire, from bonnets and gloves to bodices and boots. As she flipped through the pages, she could imagine it on a shelf in the library where visitors to the B&B might find it interesting. She took it with her.

Past the books, she spied a few aisles filled with toys, both modern and vintage. Radio controlled cars sat next to wooden hobby horses, and modern board games were stacked next to a range of dolls from yesteryear. Maris had to smile. It was both an education in current toys and a trip down memory lane. At the back, a young girl was trying a hula hoop under her mother's supervision.

Finally though, Maris reached the stairs and, with Aurora nowhere in sight, she decided to climb.

Unlike the first floor, which had been an open area, the second story contained hallways, rooms and suites. Men's suits, dress shirts, and ties occupied the first room, along with tuxedos and dinner jackets. Other rooms held ball gowns and evening dresses, as well as slacks, business suits, and blouses. Several women were browsing the racks of casual wear. Then came the children's clothing.

"Amazing," Maris said.

Like Aurora herself, it was an eclectic and beautiful selection of goods.

Once again at the end of the floor, she took the stairs.

Rooms and hallways marked the third floor as well, but larger this time—maybe former presidential suites. This was apparently the furniture level. Different areas displayed furnishings for different rooms of a home—inlaid dining room tables and elegant chairs, canopied beds and convertible sofas, all in styles from rustic to modern Danish. A young couple was trying out a sectional couch, and some kids were playing hide and seek among the recliners. But as Maris moved on and the sound of their laughter faded, she heard a familiar voice—and the one she'd been hunting. When she turned the corner, she saw that she'd found the appliance section.

Aurora, dressed in a plum colored, floor length skirt, and violet jacket with long, Oriental sleeves, was talking with a middle-aged couple among the outdoor grills. As she had last evening, she also wore a head wrap, which accentuated her elaborate makeup.

"We're having a family reunion in a couple of weeks," the man with a receding hairline said. "Relatives coming from all over. First time we've hosted such a thing."

"We don't want to take any chances," the woman said. "We don't want anything to go wrong."

The man nodded. "The old grill–"

"Cannot be trusted," Aurora finished for him. "All things have a useful life."

"We want something that will cook more evenly," the woman said.

Again the man nodded. "Not something

that burns steaks on the edges but leaves them rare in the middle."

Aurora indicated the large gleaming grill in front of them, its cover finished in brick red enamel. "You need look no further. Six burners, thirty-thousand BTUs, propane fuel, with electronic ignition." She rolled open the cover. "Two shelves, self-cleaning, a built-in rotisserie, and a warming area on the side. You can cook eight steaks at a time, with room to spare for corn on the cob, burgers, and hot dogs. Presto, just like that."

The man's eyes lit up. "How much is this one?"

Aurora picked up the price tag from where it was tied to one of the burner dials. She showed it to them. The man gave a low whistle. "We hadn't really counted on spending that much."

"But you are interested in quality," Aurora said to them.

"Definitely," the man answered, "it's just that..."

"It's so beautiful," his wife said. "And we wouldn't have to worry."

"Picture it in your backyard," Aurora said, "or the garden, or on the patio. Simply add this to your get-together, and presto, you are entertaining." She paused for a moment. "The price includes delivery."

"I like it," the woman said. She looked at her husband. "Up to you, honey."

He gazed longingly at it, then burst into a smile. "Let's do it." Without another word, he took out his wallet and handed over his credit card.

Maris's eyebrows rose. *That was quick.*

"Thank you," Aurora said, leading them to the cash register where she rang up the purchase. Maris followed at a discreet distance but hung back so as not to be seen.

But when the couple departed with their receipt, Aurora closed the cash register drawer and looked directly at her, though she was partially hidden by a refrigerator.

"Good morning," Aurora said to her. "Are you shopping or just...listening?"

Maris grinned and stepped out. "Both," she said, showing her the book she'd selected. "Good morning."

Aurora took it and looked at the price. "A fine choice," she said. She opened the front flap and showed Maris the row of numbers at the bottom of the copyright page. She pointed to the number one. "First edition."

"Oh," Maris exclaimed. "How nice." She took the wallet from her purse. "You have a *wonderful* shop here. I can't believe the enormous selection." She handed over the credit card. "I also can't believe this is my first visit. It certainly won't be my last."

"Thank you," Aurora said, smiling broadly and inclining her head. "Aurora appreciates your kind words—and your timing."

Maris had to grin. "I'd be lying if I said I wasn't interested in what happened last night."

Aurora gave her back her card, as well as a pen and a receipt. "Naturally."

"Ms. Puddlefoot," said a man's voice. "And Maris." She turned to see Mac McKenna approaching. "Why am I not surprised to find you here," he said to her.

"Because I have discerning taste." She took the book from the counter and showed it to him. Aurora handed her the receipt, which she tucked between the pages.

"Ah," Mac said, smiling. "Of course."

Then he turned to Aurora. "Would you mind answering a few questions about last night?"

"Of course," she said. "Aurora has been expecting you."

Maris watched as Mac processed Aurora's third person referral to herself. "You've been expecting me?"

"Aurora, after all, was one of the attendees. And she did have a row with that awful man."

Maris smiled. "Then I'll be on my way."

"No need to leave on Aurora's account," the woman said. "She has nothing to hide and no secrets..." She glanced at Mac. "At least not concerning last evening."

Of course, Maris would like nothing better than to stay, but she also didn't want to overstep her bounds.

Mac must have seen her hesitate. "If Ms. Puddlefoot doesn't mind," he said, "I don't mind. You were a witness as well."

"In that case," Aurora said, "That settles it."

10

———

Maris and Mac followed Aurora to her office, which seemed to have been one of the few rooms of the inn to have been preserved as a suite. Located at the front of the building, its tall, narrow windows looked down on the Towne Plaza. Though the gabled roof gave the room a slanted ceiling between the windows, that was the only trace of its Victorian origin. They'd entered into the sitting room of the suite, which had been completely modernized and updated as an office. Sleek desks and chairs with a minimalist design were accompanied by computers, printers, a xerox machine, and a water cooler. Two employees, who sat at the computers, looked up as they entered.

"Aurora would like to be undisturbed in the break room," she said to them, and they simply smiled and nodded before getting back to work. As she ushered the sheriff and Maris into an adjoining kitchen, Aurora said, "The bookkeeper and Aurora's secretary."

A few round, gleaming white tables with matching chairs occupied one half of the room, while the far wall had a refrigerator, shelves of glass containers with snacks of all types, and a sink and counter with a coffee maker and hot water pot.

"Aurora would like some tea," she said, gesturing for them to sit. "Would you like tea, coffee, water or a soda?"

"Tea sounds lovely," Maris answered, taking a seat.

"No thank you," Mac said, going to the tall windows and looking down.

Maris regarded the exotically dressed woman amid the white minimalism. "I must say Aurora, your offices aren't exactly what I'd expected."

The store owner filled a glass teapot with an infuser and hot water. "Perhaps you thought to find gypsy wagons and crystal balls."

Maris laughed. "Not exactly," she said, though she wouldn't have been surprised either.

The sheriff turned from the window and took the notepad from his breast pocket. "Let's begin with the argument between you and Langston Spaulding last night at the art exhibit."

Aurora brought the teapot to the table where Maris sat. "Aurora has a temper. She readily admits that, and sometimes it gets out of control." She returned to the counter and took two glass mugs and a small container of sugar packets, honey sticks, and plastic stirrers.

"Is that what happened at the exhibit?" Mac asked.

"There were, shall we say, extenuating circumstances," the shopkeeper said as she returned to the table and set down the cups and condiments.

"And what would those have been?" Mac asked.

Aurora poured two cups of tea. "That wasn't Aurora's first run-in of the day with Langston Spaulding. He and his wife were here mid-morning."

Maris took a little sniff from her cup: Earl Grey with its spicy citrus aroma. She selected one of the honey sticks, snapped it open, and poured it in.

"Why were they here?" Mac asked, walking over to the table, though he remained standing.

"To shop, of course." Aurora took a seat. "His wife perused several of the ladies' fashion rooms, particularly the evening dresses." She sipped her tea and looked at Maris. "The woman has excellent taste in clothing, if not men," she said, almost as an aside. "Unfortunately her husband was with her. It was a mistake to allow him in."

"What did he do?" Maris asked.

"He mocked Aurora's merchandise. He criticized everything. The words 'junk' and 'trash' were bandied about." She set her tea down and cupped her hands around it. "Other customers noticed him, and were put off." She jutted out her chin as she looked up at Mac. "Aurora is the owner and sole proprietor of Magical Finds and reserves the right to deny service to anyone at any time." With a little nod, she added, "Aurora told him to leave."

"And what did he do?" Mac asked.

"The boor refused," she said, her voice rising. "Refused! It was then that he became highly insulting to Aurora personally. As Aurora told Maris, he asked her if her makeup was inspired by Ronald McDonald or Bozo."

Mac's eyebrows rose as he made a note. "I assume he did leave though."

"Only because his wife did," Aurora said, calming down. "That poor woman was so embarrassed and uncomfortable. She almost ran from the shop. He had no choice but to follow her."

Based on what little Maris had observed of them together, and Jayde alone, she could easily picture it.

"The art exhibit," Mac said, as he finished jotting down a note. "That was the next time you saw him."

"Yes," she said grimacing. "He was berating Clio Hearst's work. In Aurora's opinion, Clio is a very talented artist. In fact, you may have noticed that several of Clio's paintings are on display at Magical Finds."

"I saw them on the first floor," Maris said.

Aurora nodded. "She's an excellent artist who barely scrapes by. She makes ends meet by teaching art, both in Pixie Point Bay and in Cheeseman Village."

"Her art was on exhibit," Mac said, bringing the discussion back on point.

"Aurora was looking at it when that boor came up to her and asked why she was spending time with the doodlings of a child." Her voice was rising again. "Aurora should have walked away from him, but she was still angry about their earlier encounter. It's one thing to attack Aurora, and another to attack someone she admires. Words were said. Accusations were flung. In hindsight Aurora realizes that the fool was being purposefully annoying."

"And what happened next?" the sheriff asked.

"The art dealer who represents Clio, the Russian man, he tried to intervene. For his trouble, he got a bloody nose." She took a sip of her tea.

"Mikhail Galkin," Maris said. "Do you know who hit him?"

The shopkeeper shook her head, making her platinum braids sway. "Aurora truly doesn't know. It happened in the heat of the moment, and very quickly."

Maris noted that Mikhail had said virtually the same thing.

Mac nodded. "That was the last time you saw Langston Spaulding?"

"Him, yes," Aurora agreed, "but not the wife. Afterward, Aurora went to the ladies room to…freshen her makeup." She looked at Maris. "We were in conversation for a few minutes before Jayde Spaulding barged in."

"Barged in?" Mac said, looking at them both.

Maris frowned a little. "She was in a hurry, it seemed, but then she left in a hurry as well."

"When she saw Aurora," the shopkeeper said, "she quickly left." She paused for a moment eyeing the sheriff's notepad. "So in case you're thinking of Aurora as a suspect, she has two witnesses that saw her in the bathroom."

Mac shook his head as he closed the notepad. "Although Mr. Spaulding's death might have been instantaneous, the coroner has given me a two hour range for when it happened." He tucked the pad back in his pocket. "Anyone at the gala could have done it."

"Oh," Aurora said, looking down into her tea.

He inclined his head to them. "Thank you both for your time," he said with a smile, then checked his watch. "I've got to get to my appointment with Ms. Hearst." He took a business card from his other pocket. "If you remember anything else, I'd appreciate it if you let me know."

Aurora took the card but gaped at him. "Clio Hearst? Surely you don't think an artist could have done it. And certainly not Clio, with her...well, her artistic sensitivity."

"But she *is* an artist," Mac said.

Maris's eyebrows drew together as she looked up at him. "Does being an artist have something to do with the murder?"

The sheriff nodded. "It does in this case. The murder weapon was a painting knife."

11

———

On her way back to the B&B, Maris stopped at Flour Power Sandwiches & Gas Station to kill two birds with one stone. A visual throwback to the 50s, the red vintage gas pumps were in the shadow of a large red and white striped awning which was an extension of the roof. Matching candy apple red doors and window frames fronted the small sandwich shop, and the attached garage and maintenance bay's roll-up door was also red.

Although Maris had known the place since she was a child, the former owners had long since retired. Maris's Aunt Glenda had been good friends with the older couple, and she wondered if that didn't explain the paperwork she'd found in her aunt's pretty brocade box. Along with the deed to the property and the generous life insurance policy that had benefitted both her and Cookie, she also found a promissory note. Glenda had apparently helped to fund the transfer of the business to the new owners, Jude and Fabiola Toussaint, recent arrivals from Haiti.

As Maris pulled up to the pump, Jude emerged from the open garage bay, wiping his hands with a rag. "Good to see you, Ms. Seaver. Fill her up?"

Tall and slender but with wide shoulders, Jude was in his early thirties and the picture of radiant health. He wore his dark hair cropped short, and his black eyes glittered almost as brightly as his big and brilliant smile.

"Jude," she said getting out of the car. She put her hands on her hips and gave him a mock scowl. "We've been over this. It's Maris."

He laughed, his bass voice rumbling a bit. "Yes, ma'am...er, Maris."

"Good," she said. "And yes, please. Fill it

up." She reached inside and popped the tank cover.

As she watched him unscrew the cap, she said. "I need your advice about something."

"Name it," Jude said, grabbing the pump's nozzle.

"This car's a rental," she said looking at the compact. "When I was globetrotting for the job, I gave up having a car. It was more trouble than it was worth. But now that I'm settled…"

"You're thinking of buying something?" Jude asked as he inserted the nozzle and started the gas.

"Sort of," she said. "The thing is, we have a vehicle at the B&B."

Jude nodded. "Ah yes. I remember Glenda's truck."

Maris grimaced a little. "That's the one. It hasn't even been started for months."

The gas nozzle clicked off, and Jude removed it. "That's not too good," he said. "I doubt that it will run."

"That's pretty much what I was thinking," Maris agreed.

"I'd be glad to come over and take a look

at it," he said, replacing the pump nozzle and smiling at her. "Just let me know what day and time would be good."

"Oh, thank you, Jude," she said, exhaling. "You're a lifesaver." She opened the car door as he put the cap back on. "I'm going to pick up some of your wife's wonderful sandwiches. Can I pay for everything inside?"

"Absolutely," he said. "Just let Fab know."

Maris parked the compact in one of the parking spots in front of the sandwich shop and headed inside—and instantly saw they'd redecorated. As far as the location of the counter and the general layout of the high tables and stools, little had changed. But the decor was now a radical departure from the 50s look outside. It was as though the Mexican Day of the Dead was celebrated all year.

Vibrantly colored miniature skulls dotted the shelves, accompanied by candles and small vases of flowers. On the walls were neon paintings on black velvet that looked like people Maris ought to know—holding items of apparent significance or wearing special hats and jewelry. Yet she didn't recognize a single one. Nor did she really think that the skulls and candles were a tradition from Mexico. More than likely they came from Haiti, like the Toussaints, and might possibly be related to the voodoo—or vodun as they called it—that Maris had learned that they practiced.

"Maris," the woman behind the counter said. "Good morning." Fabiola was as beautiful as her husband was handsome. With straight hair that fell almost to her trim waist, and just a touch of makeup, she could easily have been a supermodel. Her incredible smile was the icing on the cake.

"Good morning, Fab," Maris said, smiling in return. She gestured to the shop. "I adore this new look."

"Thank you," she said. "I thought it was time for a little touch of home." She paused for a moment and then looked Maris in the eye. "You know who first suggested it? Your aunt."

"Really?" Maris said, giving it a new look. "Well, kudos to Aunt Glenda. It's looking positively magical."

Fabiola smiled knowingly. "Can I get you a cup of coffee?"

Maris shook her head. "I'm afraid I've

reached my caffeine limit for the day. But I would like to order some sandwiches to go."

"Wonderful," she said. "What can I make for you?"

Maris looked up at the menu board. Not only were there different types of sandwiches, customers had their choice of bread, all kinds of condiments, plus a selection of fresh vegetable toppings. It was a bit overwhelming.

"Is there something in particular that you could recommend?" Maris asked.

"I have just this very minute finished making both tuna salad and egg salad. Maybe those two?"

Maris nodded. "That sounds like a winner. Maybe three of each."

"Coming right up," Fab said.

As Maris waited, she glanced at the rental car parked outside and a new thought occurred to her. "I'm just going to go ask Jude a quick question," she told Fab. "Be right back."

"Sure thing," she called back.

Maris headed through the door that connected the shop to the garage—but it was empty except for an enormous gold Cadillac El Dorado.

"Jude?" Maris said.

"Maris?" he said, his voice muffled and coming from under the car. She crouched down and peered underneath it. He was lying on his back on a rolling board, and their adorable dachshund was next to him. The little wiener dog gave a yelp, and tried to run to Maris, though the short legs gave him a decidedly lopsided gate.

"Gherkin," she said, clapping her hands. "Come here, boy."

Although he collided with her ankles, he seemed not to notice and instead flopped onto his back to have his stomach scratched.

Jude rolled himself out from under the car and sat up, eyeing the dog. "Watch out for the shop's attack dog."

Maris laughed. "I have subdued said attack dog with belly rubs." She glanced at the big Caddy. "Am I interrupting you?"

"Not at all," he said as he stood and wiped his hands on an rag. "This old hog is a work in progress."

"Okay," she said, still rubbing Gherkin's belly. "I was wondering if it's really worth getting the old pickup running. I'm not particularly fond of trucks. So maybe I should just buy a new car. Or maybe a used one—except that I don't want to get stuck with a clunker."

"I *always* prefer used cars," he said.

Maris's eyebrows arched. "Really. Why is that?"

"When you buy a new car, you're paying for the newness." He tossed the rag onto a nearby tool bin. "As soon as the tires leave the lot, you can expect the value to drop right there and then."

"So it's a waste of money."

He shook his head. "It all depends. I have customers who lease, and never want to own. They like having the latest model and the latest gadgets. The car means a lot to them." He watched Gherkin lay placidly on his back. "It's not a waste of money if the car is important. Is a car important to you?"

Maris gave Gherkin a final pat and stood up. "No. I'm afraid it's not. Not only do I not know the first thing about them, but I haven't owned one for years, or been able to keep track of all the new gadgets. At this point, it's just a way for me to get around and shop for the B&B."

"Then I'd like to recommend looking for a used car," he said, picking up Gherkin.

"Good for the bank account, and good for the planet."

Maris grinned at him. "You've convinced me." She watched him give Gherkin a gentle scratch under the chin. "I guess I'd better start looking in the paper."

"There's no need for that," he said, as they walked toward the sandwich shop door. "I get a constant stream of car owners who are getting their vehicles ready to trade in, or sell themselves. If you're willing to wait for a bit, I'm sure I'll come across something."

Maris could have hugged him. "Really? Well that would be perfect." It was a no-brainer. There was no one she'd trust more about vehicles than Jude.

"Once I get the truck running," he said as they stopped at the door, "I'm sure I can find a buyer for that too. There's actually quite a bit of demand for trucks like that."

She opened the door to the sandwich shop. "Did anyone ever tell you you're a nice man?"

Jude laughed but Fab must have heard them. "I have," she called out to Maris. She waved a receipt in the air. "Your sandwiches are ready."

"Perfect," Maris said.

Jude held the door open for another second and Gherkin peeked inside. "You have a great day, Maris."

"I think I already have," she said, grinning.

12

Back at the B&B, Maris noticed that there were no cars parked outside. No doubt the Schellings were out trying to get a photo of Claribel. As she brought in the sandwiches, she decided that Mikhail might have some organizing to do at Inklings to get the exhibit packed away. Of course the Spaulding's car was absent as well. Since Jill had brought Jayde back to the B&B last night, her car would still be in town. Fetching it would probably not be high on the list of priorities. Hopefully Jayde was resting upstairs.

Since it wasn't quite lunchtime, Maris stowed the sandwiches in the fridge. She peeked out back and saw that Cookie and Bear were taking advantage of the warm and sunny day to work in the herb garden. Maris, however, had a list of chores that took place inside. Then again, she didn't want to make a lot of noise if Jayde was finally resting. Quietly, she went upstairs to check on her. But to Maris's surprise, the door to her room was open and she was gone.

"Hmm," she muttered, frowning. Perhaps Mikhail had given her a ride to pick up her car. But since the B&B appeared to be empty, now was the time to get a few things done.

Downstairs, she started a load of wash before she fetched the vacuum from the utility room and ran it through the guest rooms and hallways upstairs first, before anyone returned. She turned down all the beds, and saw that Cookie had already cleaned the bathrooms and set out fresh towels and toiletries. Before she finished upstairs, she quickly fetched a garbage bag and gathered up all the trash, before bringing it and the vacuum cleaner downstairs.

On the first floor, she moved the washed sheets and towels to the dryer. Then she dusted all the public rooms first, and was about to finish by running the vacuum through them when she passed the parlor for maybe the twentieth time. Except now Mojo was on the Ouija board.

She came to an immediate stop and backed up a pace. His big orange eyes had that strange faraway stare. With the exception of his ears, which continually cocked in every direction, he sat so still that not even his tail twitched. For all the world he looked exactly as though he was listening to the spirits.

"Here we go," Maris muttered to herself, as she went in to watch.

In the beginning, she had assumed that when Mojo played with the planchette, he was doing just that—playing. But over time she'd come to realize that what he did wasn't random at all. Perhaps he played in the parlor at other times when she hadn't watched. But every time she'd seen him on the Ouija board, he'd spelled something relevant, if not inscrutable.

In silence, she approached the board so she could see through the clear part of the planchette, and watched in fascination as Mojo gently put his paw on it. Slowly it moved over the letter A at the far edge of the board. Then he moved it to the center.

"T," Maris whispered.

With a quick movement, he almost seemed to flick it over the R.

Maris scowled at him. A, T, R?

But he wasn't through. Moving slowly again, his paw seemed to ride the gliding planchette to a stop over the I, then the U almost below it in the second row, and then the M.

"Atrium," Maris murmured. She frowned. "Atrium?" What did an atrium have to do with anything, particularly murder at an art exhibit?

Although she waited on the off chance that perhaps there'd be another word, Mojo was done. He stood, shook out his fur, and lightly jumped to the floor.

As he bounced past her, she said to him, "Atrium? Really?" But without so much as a backward glance, he trotted down the hall. "Thanks," she called out after him.

13

The rumbling of Maris's stomach signaled the arrival of lunch. She fetched the sandwiches from the refrigerator along with a pitcher of iced tea. After loading them and three glasses on a tray, she headed to the back porch.

In the herb garden, Bear was following Cookie with a potted plant in each hand. As usual, their bearded handyman wore a plain white t-shirt under blue bib overalls, neither of which did much to hide his massive size and burgeoning middle. Maris set down the tray and descended the steps to the grassy area.

"Good afternoon, you two," she said. "Lunch is served."

Cookie smoothed some hair out of her

face with the back of her gloved hand. "That sounds good," she said. She glanced up at Bear who had immediately focused on the tray, though he still held the pots of what looked like rosemary. "You can set those down right there, Bear," she told him. "Let's eat."

He did exactly as he was told, but politely waited for Cookie to precede him. As she headed down the row to where Maris waited, she took off her gloves and lightly tossed them into a bucket.

"I guess Jayde won't be joining us," the chef said.

Maris climbed the porch steps with her. "I saw that she was gone, and Mikhail as well."

"There was some paperwork at the coroner's office," Cookie said, "and he was kind enough to take her."

"Oh," Maris said, as they took a seat. Although she'd hoped there might be a more upbeat reason for the poor woman to have gone out, paperwork unfortunately made sense. Insurance companies, banking institutions, even lawyers and the government were all going to get involved. It'd taken her and Cookie months to sort everything out, despite the fact that Glenda had left so much in order.

Cookie poured three iced teas as Maris unpacked the sandwiches. "I've tried a new sun-brewed recipe," the herb gardener said. "But I haven't tasted it yet."

Although Bear had been watching the sandwiches intently, all three of them now focused on the glasses. As though they were a synchronized tasting team, they picked up their drinks and took a sip.

"Oooh," Maris said. "That is really wonderful. Black tea with a hint of...lemon?" She took another sip. "Mmm, yes, that's so refreshing."

Bear gave an appreciative "Ahh," as he set down his glass, now half-empty. "It's good."

Cookie smiled as she finished her taste. "I'm glad you both enjoy it." She regarded her glass and then held it up to the sun, squinting at it. "I think it turned out rather well."

As Maris unpacked the sandwiches, she said, "Rather well? I hope you've kept the recipe." She placed the foil and paper wrapped sub sandwiches in two piles. "Egg salad and tuna salad. Fresh from the sandwich board of Fabiola Toussaint."

"There are six," Bear said. He glanced at the house. "Even if Jayde and Mikhail were here, that's too many."

Maris smiled at him. "There are always two for you, Bear." She looked at Cookie. "I don't have a preference. Do either of you?"

Bear folded his big hands on the table in front of him. "One of each, please."

"Tuna salad and egg salad for the hungry gardener," she said, placing them in front of him.

He bobbed his big head. "Thank you."

"Tuna for me," Cookie said.

Maris scooted one over to her. "And I think I'll try the egg salad."

For a few minutes they ate in companionable silence, and Maris decided that the egg salad was nothing short of a work of art. Not only was the balance of mayo and mustard just right, Fab had added diced celery for a wonderfully crunchy texture, and spices that brought out the creamy but nutty flavor of the yolk. Was that a hint of curry that she tasted?

"Mmm," Bear said, already halfway through his first sandwich.

Cookie paused to pull out the tiny whole

pickle that was part of each and every sand-wich that the shop made. "I've never under-stood this," the chef said. "But I like it." She smiled and took a crisp bite.

As Maris settled back and took another sip of the iced tea, she remembered Mojo's Ouija clue. Although she pondered it, nothing that related to the case occurred to her.

"Say, you two," she said. "Let me pass something by you."

"Shoot," Cookie said, taking a napkin.

"Does the word 'atrium' mean anything to you?"

Cookie laughed. "Only that I've always wanted one." She looked behind her at the B&B. "A glass covered one, of course. It'd be wonderful to have a sheltered place to start new seedlings, and a central courtyard in the house would be fabulous." She turned back to them. "But not only is the B&B perfect as it is, it's a registered historical building, so there's no way we're going to be putting in an atrium."

Bear was opening his second sandwich but stopped. "Does it have to be in the house?"

"An atrium?" Cookie asked.

"No," he said, "the glass." He pointed at a spot just beyond the herb garden. "If you want a glass house, I can build one there."

Cookie sat bolt upright, her eyes wide. "What did you say?"

Bear pointed again. "I can build a glass house."

Cookie put a hand to her chest. "Well, I...I think that'd be wonderful." She looked at Maris. "What do you think?"

Maris made a show of peering at the spot. "I think a Victorian hot house would be a great addition." She nodded. "Very authentic."

Cookie clapped her hands once. "I've always wanted one," she exclaimed.

Bear resumed unwrapping his second sandwich just as the dryer in the utility room gave its end-of-cycle ding.

Maris jumped up. "I forgot," she said. "I put that–"

Cookie took hold of Maris's chair. "You sit down, young lady, and finish your lunch."

In mid-bite, Bear flicked his eyes between the two of them.

"But I'm finished with my lunch," Maris said. "I'm just going to–"

"Finish your tea, then," Cookie said, pointedly looking at it. "It won't take long."

Although Maris was tempted to simply gulp it down and go, she knew what Cookie had in mind. Not only had Maris's aunt died of a heart attack, but her mother as well. All the women in her family had seemed to struggle with their weight and cholesterol. Not only that, they'd all suffered from the same crazy Type A work ethic, though Maris classified herself as Type A+.

As Cookie picked up her sandwich, and Maris sat back down, the chef said, "What have you done to slow down today?"

The question almost didn't make sense. Wasn't doing something the opposite of slowing down? But Maris knew that she wasn't going to let her off the hook. From trying to switch from coffee to tea, and learning to simply let the tea brew in its own good time, Cookie had been trying to chip away at Maris's obsessive need to be busy. She did some quick thinking.

"I thought I might take an art class with Clio Hearst," she said.

Cookie's eyebrows rose, and Maris was aware that Bear was watching both of them.

"An art class," Cookie said slowly. "Hmm." She narrowed her eyes. "This wouldn't have anything to do with investigating the death of Langston Spaulding, would it?"

Maris tilted her head. "Well, obviously that's how I came to learn that she teaches in Cheeseman Village and in town," she admitted. "But maybe it's time I tried to find a hobby." She looked from Cookie to Bear. "Bear has his beekeeping when he's not here." The big man gave a single nod. "And you have your gardening," she told the chef. "Maybe I can learn watercolors."

"Good," Cookie said with a little smile. "I think that's a great idea."

Maris took a sip of her tea, and suddenly remembered the conversation with Jude.

"By the way," she said, "while I was picking up the sandwiches, I was chatting with Jude about trying to get the old truck started. I don't think it makes sense for me to keep driving a rental."

Cookie paused. "You're going to drive that big old thing?"

"Actually, no. Jude thinks he might be able to sell it. Then I'll buy something used from him, and turn in the rental. But I wanted to run it by you first, of course. I know you and Aunt Glenda shared it."

Cookie shook her head. "I'm not interested in driving it, much less hauling heavy gardening supplies anymore."

Bear wiped his mouth and beard with his napkin. "I can do the hauling."

Cookie smiled at him, reached out, and touched his arm. "Don't ever leave, Bear."

As though she'd been perfectly serious, he said, "I won't."

Maris grinned at them both. "It's settled then. I'll let Jude know."

14

———

Maris finished folding the sheets and towels and stacked them all neatly before she went to her room and booted up her rarely used laptop. Although she'd lugged it around the world a couple of times, it'd never really been her tool of choice for staying in touch. A phone call had always been faster and easier. But for research, it couldn't be beat.

In under a minute, she had her information. Clio Hearst was offering a watercolor class in Cheeseman Village that started tomorrow. The artist's web site named the supplies each student would need and listed three or four places that sold them. The closest was Robbie's Hobbies, located in the Pixie Point Bay Towne Plaza.

She grabbed her purse and went back into the house. Although she'd been about to head out to the garden, she found Cookie in the kitchen emptying the dishwasher.

"Just wanted to let you know that one of Clio Hearst's art classes opens tomorrow in Cheeseman Village. I looked it up online. And there's a list of supplies each student will need and places where you can buy them."

"So you're off on a supply run then?" the chef said, stacking some dishes on the counter.

"I am. I've just registered and paid the class fee. So I'm off to Robbie's Hobbies to buy the things I'll need."

"Good for you," Cookie said, smiling. "Have fun."

"Will do," Maris replied.

She made the short car trip from the B&B to the Towne Plaza, a pretty journey on any day, but particularly in the afternoon as dappled sunlight filtered through the oaks that lined the road. Perhaps she was thinking of Clio's watercolors, but she had the distinct feeling that she was traveling through a painted landscape of lush green countryside. By the time she arrived at the quaint plaza, she was already wondering what she herself might paint. The opportunity in the local environs were almost limitless. From the flower fields of the Pixie Petal farms, to the towering redwoods just inland, and of course the bay, there would be no dearth of interesting subjects.

But first things first, she thought, as she parked in front of Robbie's Hobbies. Not only was it time to get all the tools, it was time to pay her first visit to the town's hobby store.

Bright green wood trim surrounded the large and positively packed display windows. All three were filled with boxes of models that included planes, boats, and cars. The second story of the Victorian was finished in red brick, and the windows there were also framed in green and decorated with floral print curtains that were drawn closed.

Inside the shop, Maris paused for a few moments to get herself oriented. The small store was packed from floor to just below the ceiling, side to side, and front to back. Every imaginable type of model and train set filled the place. What quickly drew her eye, though, was the ceiling. Squadrons of completed and beautifully detailed airplanes were suspended from it. Some flew in tight formation, while others seemed to be flying solo, headed in different directions.

Maris smiled at the myriad styles and time periods as well, from the triple-winged Red Baron to a space shuttle.

"Wow," she muttered.

"Hello," a voice said, "and welcome." Maris turned to find a man behind a glass counter that she hadn't noticed, likely because the display case was full of miniature trees, people, and buildings, and the wall behind the man was completely full of bins that held balsa wood, paper, and metal cans of glue.

In fact, as Maris approached the man, the distinct smell of airplane glue became more and more apparent. The tall thin man who'd greeted her was working on what appeared to be a World War II bomber.

"Can I help you find something?" he asked.

Maris guessed he might be in his sixties, short cropped gray hair, and his brown eyes the size of saucers behind the magnifier headset he wore. Bright red suspenders held up his pants.

"Hello," Marilyn said. "I'm looking for watercolor painting supplies."

"Ah," he said, taking off the magnifiers. "You'll be taking one of Clio Hearst's art classes."

"I will indeed," Maris said, surprised. "How did you know?"

His smile broadened as he picked up a flyer and handed it to her. "Clio buys many of her own supplies here, which is why she recommends me."

"Oh," Maris said, as he came around the counter. "Excellent."

"Right this way," he said.

She followed him through the maze of kits and supplies, past a section filled with small bits of electronics, and finally to the fine art section. As with the rest of the store, there was a bewildering array of choices. She glanced at the flyer and then at the papers, brushes, and paints.

"Shall I pick out her recommendations?" he asked.

Maris exhaled and smiled. "I'd appreciate that."

As he selected a block of watercolor paper, he said, "You live around here?" He handed it to her.

"Yes," she said, taking the block and extending her other hand. "Maris Seaver."

He paused and turned to her. "Seaver?" He shook her hand. "Related to Glenda?"

Maris smiled. "Her niece. I'm running the B&B and lighthouse now."

"Robbie Grayson," he said smiling. "At your service. I'm glad to see the place stay in the family."

"Pleased to meet you, Robbie, and thanks."

Next he selected the paintbrushes, and then a tray of pigments with a metal lid that he popped open. On its underside were small depressions. "The lid doubles as a paint tray," he explained. "One less thing to buy."

"Very nice," Maris said. She held out the paper block, and he put the paint and brushes there.

As they went back to the register, he said, "Bad business about that art critic."

Maris nodded. "Very," she said and glanced out a front window. "I hope that Alfred and Minako are getting back to normal."

"For sure," he said, ringing up her purchases. "And Clio. It's got to be hard to focus after something like that."

Maris handed him her credit card. "I'm sure that's true." She hadn't seen Clio after the murder, but could easily imagine that the artist would be shaken. In fact, now she recalled that Mikhail had said as much.

With the purchase complete, Robbie tucked the goods and the flyer in a paper bag and handed it to her. "I'm sure you'll enjoy her class."

"Thank you, Robbie," she said smiling. "I'm sure I will."

15

It was a rare evening at the B&B when there was no Wine Down. But since none of the guests had returned, Maris decided to skip the evening wine and cheese. Mikhail might still be with Jayde, and perhaps they'd found a way to keep themselves busy. More than likely though, she was still dealing with the aftermath of her husband's death. As for the Schellings, Maris hoped the young couple were enjoying themselves by checking out Claribel from a satisfying number of angles.

Cookie had retired for the evening, and Bear liked to be home before dark. So Maris wandered out to the garden in the last rays of the setting sun. The chef and her brawny helper had got a lot done. There was a new row of freshly planted herbs, including the rosemary that Bear had been carrying. In the still air of the evening, the aroma was wonderful. The red-gold light from the horizon bathed the plants in warm colors and had them casting shadows that made them seem as tall as trees. Maris took her time walking up the row, and let the tips of her fingers skim the tops of the various plants. As she brought her hand to her nose, she smiled. Not only had rosemary been planted but dill as well. She could hardly wait to find out what Cookie had planned for it.

As she gazed out at the shimmering bay, she thought back on the busy day. Though she'd been bustling from morning until now, she was nagged by the feeling that little progress had been made on the murder of Langston Spaulding. Although she'd be seeing Clio tomorrow, Maris glanced up at the lighthouse. Perhaps the Old Girl would be able to help her in the meantime.

Just before Maris reached the door, a light breeze seemed to swirl in front of it, and it swung open. Maris smiled as she stepped inside and turned on the light switch.

"Good evening, Claribel," she said, as the door closed softly behind her.

She climbed the spiral metal staircase slowly, pacing herself for the three stories of stairs to come. As she ascended, she took a moment to glance out the windows on each level. Like miniature works of art, they showed the bay and the coast, bathed in the surreal colors of the sinking sun.

By the time she reached the top, as usual, she had to pause for a breath.

"Phew!" she exhaled, and took in the panoramic view.

It wasn't often she could be up in the lighthouse's optic house at this beautiful time of day. Though she enjoyed the Wine Down and the lovely views from the B&B's bay windows, none of them could match this. It was like being on top of the world. Not a single cloud was in the sky, and its blue vault quickly turned to indigo overhead. The inky waters of the ocean glittered like black diamonds. A single small sailboat skimmed the water below, heading for the pier, and keeping well away from the rocky shore.

Claribel shone her light just a few feet above Maris's head, whirling in her continuing responsibility to keep sailors like the ones below safe. Even through Glenda's death and the fire in the base of the tower, the Old Girl had never missed a day on the job. Bear had cleaned the smoky haze from the fresnel lens and restored it to its pristine glory. The lens itself was more like a sculpture than a simple piece of glass. It was shaped like a giant egg, with dozens of individual pieces of glass, some grooved with concentric circles, fitted together on a gleaming steel frame. It rose from its waist high pedestal up to nearly the top of the circular glass house.

Careful to avoid the beam, Maris looked into the glass base and past the surface. A rainbow of glittering sparkles danced within the clear glass, as though a dozen prisms were scattering the light. But as she watched, a faint image began to form. It was the bookstore and there was Mikhail. He was dismantling the exhibit and carefully packing up the paintings. Despite having the help of a few workers, he looked a bit harried, as well as tired.

Suddenly, Claribel zoomed in on one of the paintings that had yet to be packed. It was that strange portrait of a nurse, the one that Jill Maxwell had been near. The subject wore a vintage white nurse's uniform and hat, and a surgical mask covered her mouth and nose. At the top of the painting were the words "Pedigreed Nurse," as though it was some type of pulp fiction cover.

"What in the world?" Maris muttered, just as the vision winked out.

She recalled the painting, of course, and yet what it had to do with Langston Spaulding she couldn't fathom. As the last glimmer of direct sunlight faded behind her, Maris sighed.

"Thanks, Old Girl," she murmured, and then gave the base of the lens a gentle pat.

16

"You're sure?" Maris asked.

Cookie smiled, and made a shooing motion with her spatula. "I'm almost finished," she said. "Going classic today after the Breakfast Pie: eggs scrambled with Parmesan and basil; bagels with onions, lox, and cream cheese; and country potatoes with red and green peppers and just a touch of garlic."

Although Maris needed to leave early for her art class in Cheeseman Village and had felt bad about leaving everything to Cookie, now she felt bad about missing the wonderful breakfast. Cookie obviously had everything under control.

The chef pointed to a small plastic bag on

the counter. "Made you a bagel sandwich to go." She nodded to a travel mug. "And a morning pick-me-up tea."

Maris beamed at her. "Cookie, you are an angel in an apron."

"Remember that when you're lugging home cheese from the dairy," she said.

"Are we in need?" Maris asked, picking up her sandwich and tea. Then she opened the refrigerator for a quick check. The cheese supply was indeed running low. "Got it," she said, closing the door.

"Have a nice time," Cookie said, smiling as she turned back to the stove.

"I think I will," Maris said and really meant it.

The drive north to Cheeseman Village in the morning fog was a slow one, but uneventful. She sipped her tea as she crossed the dramatic Pixie Point Bridge, and munched her glorious bagel, egg and cream cheese sandwich as she headed inland and into the morning sun. The black and white dairy cows dotted the grassy landscape, their heads low, having their own breakfast. Maris smiled at a pair of young calves who seemed to be frolicking by kicking up their heels.

On the old fashioned main street, where only a few cars were parked at diagonals, the stores were quiet except for the coffee and pastry shop. A couple of people were walking their dogs, but the village had an early morning "stillness before the bustle" feel that Maris used to enjoy in her hospitality days.

Finally though, her GPS navigated her to the Cheeseman Village high school. There was plenty of parking in the lot and, since Maris had left herself extra time on her first trip to the school, she decided to find the classroom early and not be in a rush. She checked the flyer in her paper bag of supplies, found the room number, and headed to the buildings.

To her pleasant surprise, she was the first student to arrive for the class, where she found the instructor distributing jars of water around the room.

"Good," Maris said, "I found the right place ."

Clio looked up, her brows arching as she smiled. "Maris Seaver, what a wonderful surprise." She looked past her through the door. "You didn't bring that wonderful lighthouse with you, did you?"

Maris laughed. "If only I could," she said, setting down the bag. "Then again, it's foggy at the bay, so I'm afraid she's needed there."

Clio gave her a little smile. "She," the artist said. "That's funny, because I think of her that way too."

Maris nodded. "She has a way of growing on you." She glanced around the room. "Is there something I can help you with?"

"Sure," she said. "Every station needs two glass jars of water, about two-thirds full." She pointed to the back of the room. "The sink is there."

As they set up each painting area at the long tables, Maris noticed Clio's slightly frazzled look. Not only were her eyes a bit puffy, her nose looked red. For a moment, she recalled Robbie's words about the sensitive artist. Then she recalled Claribel's vision of the nurse painting.

As she helped to distribute rolls of drafting tape to each place, Maris said, "Can I ask you about one of the other paintings that was at the exhibit?"

Clio began setting out a few paper towels in each painting area. "Of course. Which one?"

"There was a large painting of a nurse," Maris said. "It was in a...curious style."

Clio laughed a little. "That's a polite way of putting it." She set some paper towels in place and moved to the next chair. "Pedigreed Nurse, by Damien Previs."

"Right," Maris said, "Pedigreed Nurse. That's the one. It seemed a bit out of place."

Clio nodded. "That's Mikhail's exhibit tactic. He'll often feature the work of a famous and collectible artist in order to lure in the buyers and collectors who might see some of his lesser known artists." She indicated herself. "Like me." She continued distributing the paper towels. "It also gives them something expensive to think about, in contrast to the more affordable works."

"Did Mikhail invite Langston Spaulding too?"

Clio shrugged. "It's not like he could prevent him from coming. Mikhail says that even bad publicity is still publicity."

Maris considered that for a moment. There was more to arranging an art exhibit than met the eye. "So this artist, Damien Previs, who provides a contrast or a draw. I've never heard of him before. Are you saying his work is famous?"

"Oh yes, very. And highly, highly collectible."

"Wait," Maris said, hand on hip, "That large...I don't know if it was acrylic or oil or..."

"He typically paints in acrylics," Clio interjected.

"Okay," Maris said, "that large acrylic painting. It looked like something from the cover of an old paperback novel."

Clio nodded. "Exactly. That's precisely what it is—a recreation of a pulp fiction cover."

Maris's mouth dropped open. "It's a recreation? Of someone else's work?"

The artist chuckled. "Exactly," she said again.

Maris sputtered. "But..."

Clio finished distributing the paper towels, and began to set up her easel. "The art buying public is sometimes...hard to understand." She set up a large piece of paper and clipped it in place. "His work sells very well, often for hundreds of thousands of dollars."

Maris gaped at her. How could a giant copy of someone else's old paperback cover be worth that much money?

An older woman, presumably a student, appeared in the doorway. "Is this the water-color class?"

Clio smiled at her and gestured to the room. "You've found it. Please have a seat anywhere." Then she turned to Maris. "Thanks for your help. Looks like we're ready just in time."

As the students arrived, Maris found her own seat and took out her supplies. When the chairs were full, Clio took her place at the front of the class. After a few words of welcome, she dove into an explanation of watercolor painting and how it differed from acrylics and oils. Although Maris was fascinated, the discussion was brief.

"But you didn't come hear to listen to me talk," the artist said. "And that's not how art is learned anyway. Let's begin. We're going to paint three small triptychs by taping off our paper into three vertical panels."

The group was quiet, focusing on their work, as Clio led them through the three pieces. As they waited for the first panel to dry—a blazing red and purple sunset—they moved on to the next—a nebula at night—and laid down the water layer and some background color. While the second panel dried, they moved on to the third—a sailboat on the ocean. While that was drying, they returned to the first where the background was dried and ready for them to paint black telephone poles silhouetted against the sky. The water jars were used to rinse brushes, one for the warm colors and one for the cool.

The act of painting was loose and freeform, with an emphasis on movement, not precision, and Maris found herself completely absorbed at times, and quite relaxed. But she couldn't help but notice that when Clio wasn't talking to a student, she pressed a tissue to her nose and seemed completely lost in thought.

As her three paintings began to take shape, Maris thought back to the work of Damien Previs. She had to be missing something. Maybe recreating a book cover was harder than it looked. When Clio announced the end of the hour, it surprised her.

"Thank you, everybody," she said, with what appeared to Maris as a forced smile. "You've done wonderful work. Keep it up and practice. Next week, we'll be painting florals."

As the other students packed up their supplies and admired the work of their fellow painters, Maris purposely dawdled. Slow to stop painting and slow to pack up, she was the last student in the room. As Clio began to dump and then refill the water jars, Maris joined her.

After a few moments, she asked, "Are you okay?"

Clio plopped down into a nearby chair. "Actually, I'm not." She gave Maris a rueful look. "As if it wasn't obvious."

"Is there anything I can do to help?"

Suddenly Clio's face screwed up and, as she covered it with her hands, she began to sob. Maris immediately fetched some paper towels, sat next to her, and rubbed her back between the shoulders.

"That awful man," Clio sobbed.

"Langston Spaulding?" Maris asked.

Clio thrust her hands into her lap. "No," she said, accepting the paper towels from

Maris. "That sheriff. What was his name? McKenna." Maris's eyebrows went up. "He all but accused me of the murder." Her gaze darted to Maris. "I have no idea where that paint knife came from!" She gestured around the room. "I mean, look at what I do. There's no use for a paint knife in watercolors."

As the artist wiped her eyes and nose, Maris patted her back. "He has to question everyone. It doesn't mean you're a prime suspect."

To that, Clio could only nod. She took a deep and shaky breath, before releasing it. But she seemed to be on the verge of crying again. Robbie really had been right about the sensitive artist.

"How I miss him," she whispered.

Maris frowned as her brows drew together. "Um, the sheriff or Langston?"

Clio smiled a little, but just for a second. "No one really understood him," she said, her tone bitter.

Now Maris was utterly confused. But as she was about to ask Clio what she meant, a young man appeared in the doorway.

"Is this where the watercolor class is?" he

asked, carrying a paper bag from Robbie's Hobbies.

"Yes," Clio said, quickly wiping her nose. "We'll start in about ten minutes." She glanced at Maris. "Thank you," she said, squeezing her shoulder as she stood. "For everything."

17

Despite the small-town feel of the village itself, the Cheeseman Village Dairy was a sleekly modern building. Mostly glass, with a rakishly slanted yellow metal roof, it served not only as the dairy's center, but the village's as well.

As the glass entry doors slid open, a young woman with a tray of cheese cubes greeted Maris.

"Welcome to the Cheeseman Village Dairy," she said, wearing blue jeans, the signature bright yellow polo shirt that sported the dairy's two-cow logo, and a matching ball cap. "Would you care to sample some cheese?"

Cookie's bagel sandwich had been wonderfully filling, but sampling was a great way to learn new products. Maris paused and gazed down at the young woman's tray.

The server smiled as she pointed with a gloved hand. "Swiss, provolone, Brie, Parmesan, and our version of Gorgonzola."

Using the toothpicks from the cow-shaped holder built into the tray, Maris made her selection. "Brie contrasts nicely with the parmesan," she said, spearing one of each. "And who can resist Gorgonzola?"

The young woman beamed at her. "It's my favorite. I think I could eat my weight in it."

Maris smiled at her. "A slim thing like you can get away with that." She patted her own tummy. "But I think I'll stop with these."

"Please let any of the associates on the floor know if you have any questions," she said cheerily, as Maris turned to head into the store.

"Thank you," Maris said, and took a bite of the blue-veined Gorgonzola. "Mmm," she muttered. It was firmer than most but still creamy, with a nice amount of salt and a true bite from the veins. She'd definitely be taking some of that home.

As she fetched a shopping basket, she

took in the expansive market. It occupied the entire first floor of the building, with refrigerated cases covering each and every wall. But for once, Maris passed all these up as she made her way to the back. A small crowd was gathering at the base of the stairs that led to an observation deck on the second floor. It looked as though a tour was beginning. Without a pressing appointment or a turnover of guests at the B&B, Maris decided that today would be ideal to spend some time investigating. The dairy tour might be something that guests would be interested in seeing too.

An older man in a yellow polo shirt and cap stood next to the sign that read 'Tour Begins Here.' About Maris's height, he was plump and wore his wispy white hair in a combover. When he smiled, his rosy cheeks nearly hid his eyes.

"Welcome to the Cheeseman Village Dairy tour," he announced to the assembled group. "I'm Orson, your guide today," he motioned for them to follow him and headed up the stairs. "This way." As he climbed he said, "If you have any questions along the way— questions about what you see or what I say—

please ask. They say there is no such thing as a dumb question, only dumb answers." He glanced behind him with a grin. "So I've got you covered."

At the top of the stairs, they were met with an exhibit. Some cases appeared to have antique tools and original catalogs. One display included a life-sized porcelain milk cow in a stall, where a few kids were trying to attach the milking mechanism to its udder. Up above, dozens of plastic orange wedges were suspended from the ceiling, a flying flotilla of cheese. Maris smiled at the whimsical and playful feel of it all.

But Orson passed these up and headed directly to the immense glass windows, with their explanatory signs below them. The tour group fanned out on either side of him and looked down on the busy factory floor below. Giant vats that looked like they could be in a brewery were hooked up to large pipes leading in from the outside.

"Fresh cow's milk is piped directly into the vats," he said. "The first step is to separate the curds from the whey. By which I mean, separate the solids from the liquids." He looked at the group on either side of him.

"You might say that all of cheesemaking really amounts to removing water from the milk so that it can be preserved on a shelf."

A woman near Maris raised her hand. "Orson, if everything is made from fresh cow's milk, where do the different types of cheeses come from?"

He smiled, his eyes almost disappearing. "Good question. Once the solid cheese is separated from the water, it's all about the microorganisms that are added. It's the different bacteria used in each step of the aging process that determines the final flavor and texture."

"What is that thing?" a young boy asked, pointing to the factory floor below.

"The Big Blue Octopus," Orson answered.

A line of rollers, with rectangular loafs of newly wrapped cheese rolling along them, fed an enormous contraption that looked more like a blue spider to Maris than an octopus. Big blue tubes arched out from the center, each ending in a metal chamber for its foot. Unlike a spider though, the whole thing spun in a circle.

"That's our vacuum sealer," Orson explained. "The blocks of cheese roll in and their packaging is given an airtight seal before they roll out."

One of the workers, wearing a net over his hair and also his beard, was piling smaller blocks of cheese into stacks two high on a different assembly line. When the young boy waved at him, the young man smiled and waved back. Workers with rubber gloves, ear protection, and hair nets were working everywhere.

For a few moments they watched in silence as the Big Blue Octopus rolled out shrink-wrapped cheese, which was then swept away by a giant rotating arm into a large waiting bin with wheels. As it became full, a woman flipped a large switch, and the arm rotated in the opposite direction, sweeping the cheese blocks into a bin on the opposite side of the conveyor belt. The woman wheeled the full bin through a curtain of hanging plastic strips.

"Orson," said a man on the other side of him. "Does the dairy make any goat milk?"

The tour guide nodded. "We do. Although we're mostly a cow farm, we raise some goats for the sake of history."

"History?" someone else asked. "Is that how the dairy started?"

Orson shook his head. "Not our history, ancient history. In the Bronze age the first cheese was made from goat's milk."

The rest of the tour was as interesting as the beginning, with Orson describing the aging process, but Maris had already started considering what wine might go well with goat cheese. At the end, she thanked Orson for his informative and fascinating insights. As she descended the stairs, she was glad she had spent the time. Not only did she have a new recommendation for her guests, she hadn't known the dairy made goat cheese.

Back in the market, Maris discreetly tapped her temple to call up her photographic memory and checked the fridge. Then she did it again and checked the wine cabinet.

With an eye toward wine pairings, she slowly perused what had to be the longest cheese case in the world. Although it didn't seem to be organized in any particular way, Maris found that its seeming randomness helped her to let her creativity flow.

Without overthinking it, she selected a

nice assortment but made sure to find the Gorgonzola and the goat cheese in particular.

As she made her way to the cash registers, she passed the islands in the middle of the market, where the goods had obviously been grouped. She picked up some spicy mustard full of seeds at one, and a bag of assorted nuts at another. As she finished, she smiled to herself. The next Wine Down was going to be fun.

18

Instead of heading straight home, Maris stopped at Flour Power to let Jude know that she and Cookie had decided to sell the truck. A car was just pulling away from the gas pumps when she arrived and pulled up next to him.

"Maris," he said smiling. "I know you don't need gas, unless you've driven to Oregon and back, that is."

She laughed as she let the engine idle. "No," she said. "No gas. But I did want to let you know about the truck."

"You've made a decision," he said.

"Cookie and I have. Neither of us wants to deal with the big old thing anymore."

He nodded. "So you've decided to get rid of it."

"Exactly," she agreed. "If you can get the truck up and running and find a buyer, I'll be in the market for a used car too."

"Sounds good," he said. "I don't think I'll have a problem, with the fixing or the finding." He watched another vehicle pull in. "What time should I pick it up?"

"Any time would be fine," she said.

"I'll be by this afternoon, then." He looked at the vehicle that had pulled up next to Maris. "Good afternoon, Sheriff. You'll have to get closer if you want gas."

Maris turned to see Mac smiling at them both. "No gas today, Jude. I'm stopping by for a cup of coffee." When Maris lowered her passenger window, he said. "What a nice surprise."

"Likewise," she said.

He paused for a second and then said, "Care to join me for a cup of coffee?"

Maris felt a little teenage thrill zing down her back. The best looking boy on campus had just asked her out. "I'd be delighted!"

He grinned back at her. "Great."

He quickly parked his SUV and was at her car door before she'd even turned the engine off. When she did, he opened it for her. This was something she could get used to.

"Thank you," she said, as he lent her his hand and then closed the door, which she locked. Then he opened the door to the shop.

Inside, they were greeted by Fabiola. "Sheriff, Maris, good afternoon! What can I get for you?"

Mac looked at Maris. "Ladies first."

Maris smiled and looked up at the menu board, and then thought of the cheese she'd had at the dairy. "I think just a coffee for me."

"Coffee for me," Mac said, "and one of those bran muffins."

"For here, or to go," Fab asked.

"For here," the sheriff said, and handed her some cash. "Keep the change."

"Much appreciated," she said, inclining her head. "I'll bring it out to your table."

As they took their seats at one of the high tables, Maris noted the new paintings again. "I can't help but think I'm supposed to recognize these folks."

Mac regarded them. "You wouldn't unless you practiced voodoo."

She stared at him. "Voodoo?"

Though she'd never asked the sheriff outright, she was fairly sure that he was not one of the magic folk. But more than that, she'd learned not long after arriving back in Pixie Point Bay that the Toussaints were in fact voodoo practitioners. But the unwritten rule was that the magic folk never revealed themselves to the regular people. It was even considered bad form for one magic person to inquire about what another's gift might be. How had Mac learned that they practice voodoo?

"Actually, Fabiola says 'vodun'. She said these are the saints and spirits, aka, the *loa*."

"Really," Maris said, seeing them in a completely new light. She cast a sideways glance at Fab, who was bringing their coffees and muffin. Maris was seeing her in a new light as well. "Interesting."

"Two coffees and a muffin," the proprietor said as she set them down.

"Thanks," Mac said.

"Fab," Maris said, eyeing her. "The sheriff was just telling me about your gorgeous vodun *loa*."

"Ah, yes," she said. "We had rather a wide-ranging discussion on Haitian *art*. I credited Glenda with the idea. She was a big fan of the *art* too." She gave them both a smile. "I'll leave you two to your coffees."

As Maris watched her go, Mac took a sip of his coffee. "Are you interested in art like your Aunt?" he asked.

For a moment Maris had thought that the young couple were departing from tradition and revealing their magic ability. But really it was just as Fab had said earlier—a touch of home. As far as visitors to the shop were concerned, it was simply Haitian art inspired by the traditional heritage of voodoo there.

Maris turned back to him. "Art? No, not really," she said still thinking about Fab and Jude. Then, when she realized what she'd said, she quickly added, "Well, yes, but not particularly as a collector."

"Oh?" he said, picking up the muffin.

"Actually," she said, trying to think of how to change the subject. Then she realized that wasn't needed. "It's interesting that you ask because I took a watercolor class with Clio Hearst this morning."

"How was it?" he asked, sounding genuinely interested.

"A lot more fun than I expected," Maris

admitted. She took a sip of her coffee. "And Clio is a great teacher."

"So you're going to be the next Frida Kahlo?" he asked, nibbling on a piece of muffin.

She laughed a little. "Or maybe Grandma Moses." But she sobered as she thought of Clio sobbing. "I'm afraid Clio was very upset."

"I'm sorry to hear that," the sheriff said. "But I'm afraid I'm not too surprised. She was pretty emotional when I interviewed her. When I asked her about the painting knife, it was as if she thought I was accusing her."

"Well, actually, she told me the same thing. Is she really a suspect?"

Mac grimaced a bit and shook his head. "My gut says she's not a murderer. Sure, Spaulding attacked her work, but that seemed to be his MO with everyone."

"He really did seem very mean spirited, if you ask me."

Mac took another sip of his coffee and nodded. "And supremely unlucky, if you ask me."

"Because someone killed him for being mean-spirited?"

"Oh no. It was the way he died. A knife directly to the heart is not an easy thing to achieve. There are a lot of bones in the rib cage meant to protect the vital organs. But the thin blade of the paint knife slipped right between two and pierced Spaulding's right atrium. He died almost instantaneously."

Maris gaped at him. "Did you say atrium?"

Mac set down his coffee. "Yes," he said, his brows furrowing. "The right atrium. Why?"

She blinked recalling Mojo's Ouija clue. "Oh, um, nothing." She returned his gaze. "You're right. That was incredibly unlucky of him." Then she remembered Claribel's clue and what Clio had said about it. "Do you remember seeing a certain painting at the exhibit—the one of the nurse called 'Pedigreed Nurse'?"

Mac scowled as though he'd tasted something sour. "I do remember it. It seemed so completely out of place." He quickly held up a hand. "Not that I'm an art connoisseur, in any way, shape, or form. Why, was it something that you liked?"

She shook her head vigorously. "Oh no,

not at all. But before class, Clio was telling me that the artist, Damien Previs, sells those types of paintings for hundreds of thousands of dollars."

Mac laughed. "'The gay gaudy glare of vanity and art'." He gave her a grin.

"Robert Burns?" Maris guessed. The Scottish poet held a special place for Mac.

Mac nodded. "I think Old Rabbie had my mundane taste in art." He paused. "Even so, I find it hard to believe anyone would pay that much for that type of painting."

Just then his telephone rang, and he took it from the holder on his utility belt. "McKenna."

Though Maris couldn't have agreed more about the nurse painting, she also noted that it didn't seem to be part of Mac's investigation. But should it?

He glanced at his watch. "I'm on my way." Then he hung up. He gave Maris a sad smile. "I'm afraid I've got to go." He got up. "Please stay and finish your coffee." For a moment he looked torn, and then said, "I'm looking forward to the next time."

Maris grinned at him, that teenage shiver going down her spine again. "As am I."

19

When Maris arrived home, Bear was cutting the grass in front. As usual, he used an old push mower. Though at first Maris had thought it was a charming throwback, or maybe even Victorian gardening, he'd told her that he and Glenda had never liked all the noise of the modern ones. It was easier on the ears and also didn't disturb the guests. As she got out of the car, she appreciated it anew and waved to him. He gave his quick and almost-too-dainty wave back.

As she grabbed her paint supplies from the passenger seat, she noted that the Schellings were gone but that both Mikhail's and Jayde's cars were parked in front. He must have taken her to town to pick up the car. From the back seat, she took the two bags from the dairy, and headed into the house.

The cheese went into the fridge, the other goods into the pantry, and her paint supplies on top of her bed, where a sleepy Mojo barely raised his head to look at her.

She gently patted his warm, fluffy side. "Back to sleep," she whispered, and his head fell back to the comforter.

Despite the cars in front, the house was quiet. But when Maris checked the back porch she saw Mikhail sitting in the sun with a book. She smiled as she exited into the brightness.

He glanced up, shielding his eyes with his hand. "Maris, hello." In contrast to the tailored suit he wore at the exhibit, he had on a faded pair of jeans and a bright red t-shirt. On the table was a glass of Cookie's iced tea.

"Good afternoon, Mikhail," she said with her usual cheer. His nose was looking almost back to normal. "You're the picture of contentment."

He smiled and held up the book. "Is there anything better than a warm afternoon, a cool drink, and a good book? I almost never get a chance to do any reading. At least the ongoing investigation has given me that."

She sat down opposite him. "What are you reading?"

"A novel from the old country," he said and showed her the cover.

"*Dr. Zhivago,*" she said. Though she hadn't read the book, she'd seen the movie as a teenager. "How lovely." Then she tilted her head. "Why are you reading it in English instead of Russian?"

Mikhail smiled. "I read it as young man many years ago, in Russian of course. It is strange, but the English version feels almost as if I have never read it before." Then he gave her a wry smile. "Add to that the fact that Inklings only carried the English version."

"Ah," she said, with mock seriousness. "Now the truth comes out."

He laughed as he held the book to his chest. "I have been revealed."

She recalled the Spaulding's car out in front. "I assume Jayde is upstairs resting?"

His smile faded and he nodded. "Yes, I hope so. It has been quite awful for her, all of the legal matters and arrangements." He glanced up at the second floor of the B&B. "At least someone in the world misses him."

Maybe more than one someone, she thought, but then she spoke what he'd obviously left unsaid. "But not you."

The art dealer shrugged. "Even bad publicity is publicity, but that is all I will miss about him."

The altercation with Aurora at the exhibit, let alone Spaulding's death, had certainly provided that. For a moment she thought of the exhibit's closing and Mikhail packing up the paintings at the bookstore. "By the way," she said. "I wanted to ask you about a painting at the exhibit, the portrait of the nurse."

Mikhail perked up. "It is by the artist Damien Previs, a personal friend of mine."

"I'd never heard of him before the exhibit." Maris said.

"His work is very much in demand," the art dealer said. "At this point, he can name his price."

"Really?" she said, feigning surprise.

Mikhail nodded. "Absolutely. For example, for that particular painting I happen to know he would not part with it for less than sixty-five thousand dollars."

"Sixty-five thousand?" she said, scowling. She distinctly recalled Clio saying that they sold for hundreds of thousands of dollars.

Mikhail nodded. "If you are not active in the art world, the amounts can seem exorbitant. But collectors not only indulge their passions, they are making calculated investments."

"Investments," she muttered. "I see."

He seemed to study her and then smiled. "Care to make an offer?"

She had to laugh. Not only would she not speculate with that kind of money, but certainly not on a painting that she didn't care for. "I'm afraid it's too rich for my blood. But thanks for the opportunity." *At the reduced price*, she thought.

He shrugged. "I have a potential buyer for it in La Jolla." Then the wry smile returned. "But you could save me the cost of shipping. I can speak with Damien on your behalf."

The sound of an engine and tires on the gravel of the driveway drew her attention. It was probably Jude.

She stood and inclined her head. "I'll

keep that in mind if we ever decide to re-
decorate."

Mikhail picked up his book. "As they say
in the old country, morning is wiser than the
evening." When he saw her look of puzzle-
ment, he smiled and added, "Sleep on it."

20

Maris headed down the side of the B&B toward the front, when suddenly her surroundings disappeared. Although not quite used to the flashes of precognition to which she was prone, she at least recognized them now and managed to stop without tripping. Instead of the grassy side lawn and porch, Maris was looking at Mikhail Galkin, who she'd just left. As she watched, his hands were being put behind his back. She heard the sound of cufflinks closing. He was being arrested. But as she stared at his unhappy face, the vision winked out. In an instant, she was once again standing on the side lawn of the B&B.

She glanced over her shoulder at Mikhail, who had resumed reading. Could he really have wanted the art critic dead? Just now he'd welcomed the negative publicity, but he didn't seem to have disliked the man nearly as much as Aurora.

As Maris rounded the front of the building she spotted Jude's tow truck. He was just getting out. Bear had begun mowing the other side of the driveway.

"Long time," she said to Jude as he got out of the truck.

He laughed a little. "I've been busy."

Maris chuckled. "Shall I open the garage?"

"I'll do it," Bear said, appearing next to the tow truck. "Hi, Jude."

"Good afternoon, my friend," Jude replied smiling, as the two men shook hands. Maris noted that they were nearly identical in height, but their completely different builds had not made that apparent.

Bear opened the two wide swinging doors on the garage, which he'd already unlocked for the lawn mower. The powder blue tailgate of the old truck greeted them, just inside.

"Shall we?" Jude said to Bear, who went to the front bumper of the truck.

Maris went to the tailgate and took a grip.

"We can get it," Jude said to her. "You don't want to get dirty."

"You're right," she said. "I don't want to get dirty. But I do want to help. Call it a matter of principle."

Jude inclined his head to her. "As you wish then."

He went to the driver's door, and he cocked his head at what he saw inside. "The keys are in the ignition?"

Maris smiled at him. "We don't particularly have a problem with car theft around here. Plus the doors to the garage are generally locked so we can keep kids away from all the tools."

Jude opened the door. "I guess you always know where the keys will be." He checked Bear, and then Maris before releasing the parking brake and putting the truck in reverse. As he braced one hand on the truck's cab, he put his other on the steering wheel. "Nice and slow."

Although Maris didn't think there was any other choice, she heeded his words and didn't use all her strength to tug on the tailgate. To her shock, the truck actually moved. Slowly, the giant vehicle with its rounded fenders and back window emerged into the sun.

But when Maris paused to adjust her grip, the vehicle kept moving and she realized that her contribution was a token one at best. She looked through the cab and over the hood to see that Bear had his head down and his arms completely outstretched. He was leaning so far forward he was almost horizontal.

"That's good," Jude said, and the truck slowly came to a stop as Bear stood.

The mechanic put the column shift in park and set the brake. He closed the driver door with a solid sounding thunk. Slowly the three of them circumnavigated the vehicle. Jude ran his fingers along the fenders, actually kicked a tire, and smoothed away a fine layer of dust from the chrome rear bumper.

Jude nodded at his reflection, and they proceeded down the other side of the truck. Soon, all three of them were gathered around the front. Although a fine layer of dust covered the entire thing, Maris was relieved to see its remarkable condition. Her aunt had driven and cared for the truck as long as she could remember. She'd taken special pains to attack any rust as soon as it appeared. In the salty sea air, it'd been a constant battle.

"Nice," Jude said, swiping his hand over the hood to reveal the true lustre beneath. Then he reached under the front edge of the hood with both hands. He grinned at Bear and Maris. "The moment of truth."

Though Maris knew the giant curved hood must have weighed a ton, Jude seemed to lift it as though it were aluminum. He propped it open, stuck his head inside—and laughed.

"What?" Maris asked, her brows drawing together.

Jude reached inside, pulled something out and lightly tossed it to her.

She only just managed to control her shriek as some little furry animal flew through the air. Through sheer instinct, she managed to catch it with both hands.

"Oh, my goodness," Maris gasped, staring down at it. "It's one of Mojo's toys."

That Mojo, she thought, as she examined what appeared to be a little stuffed hedgehog. She'd never seen the same toy twice, and she had yet to discover where he kept his secret stash.

As she and Bear watched over Jude's shoulder, he poked and wiggled a few things, ducking his head left and right. Apparently satisfied, he finally stood back.

"Do you think it'll start?" Maris asked.

He nodded. "It's in much better condition than I thought it would be." He closed the hood with a heavy clunk. "But I won't try to start it now. I'd just pull all the oil that's sitting in the bottom of the pan through the engine. Time for some preventative maintenance first."

Maris exhaled with relief. "Wonderful," she said, and Bear patted the hood with a smile.

Jude took his keys from his pocket. "I'll just hook it up on the tow truck, get it back to the garage, and start work on it right away."

"There's no hurry," Maris said. "Cookie and I aren't in a rush."

He paused and smiled at her. "You're not in a hurry but the new owner is." He arched his eyebrows at her. "I've already got a buyer."

21

Back inside the B&B, Maris had to pause. She took a deep sniff.

"What is that wonderful smell?" she muttered, as she followed her nose to the only place it could be coming from. As usual, Cookie stood in front of the stove. But rather than scrambling eggs, she was stirring something in a tall iron pot.

"Cookie," Maris said, looking over the diminutive chef's shoulder. "What's this?"

"Homemade tomato soup," she replied with a smile.

Though the aroma was positively delicious, Maris stared at her. They'd settled into their routine quickly. Cookie took care of the breakfast, while Maris hosted the Wine

Down. The guests were always on their own for lunch and dinner.

"What can I say?" Cookie said, slowly stirring. "I love to cook." Then she glanced over Maris's shoulder. "And I thought maybe Jayde could use some comfort food."

"Oh how kind," Maris said, putting a hand on her shoulder. "That's so sweet of you."

"Farm fresh tomatoes, carrots, and onions," Cookie said, nodding toward the pot, "and garlic and herbs from the garden. It doesn't get any fresher."

"Or more comforting," Maris agreed.

Cookie looked over her shoulder at her. "Would you like a taste?"

Maris laughed. "I thought you'd never ask." She fetched a small spoon from the drawer, and dipped it in as Cookie stood aside. She blew on it a little, and then tasted just a bit. "Ohh," she said. "I can taste the sweetness of the tomatoes and carrots." She finished the rest of the spoon. "Mmm, yes. And the onions and garlic add just enough savory." She squinted her eyes at the pot. "It's incredibly complex." She gave the chef a smile. "Another winner."

The chef nodded at the oven, where Maris saw a loaf of bread baking. With the heady aroma of the soup, she'd completely missed the bread.

"Grilled cheese sandwiches," Cookie said, "courtesy of a recent shopping trip to the Cheeseman Village dairy."

"Perfect," Maris said.

"Speaking of Cheeseman Village," the chef said, returning her attention to the soup. "How was your art class?"

Maris smiled at her and then held up a finger. "I'll show you."

She fetched the paper block from the bag without disturbing Mojo, and brought it back to the kitchen. She opened the front cover and showed her the triptych. "This is my first attempt."

Cookie's eyes widened and she grinned. "First attempt? I'm impressed. That looks great."

"Thanks," Maris said, looking at it. "I really had a good *and relaxing* time."

Cookie laughed a little. "So you're glad you enrolled?"

Maris nodded as she set the paper block

on the counter. "I really am. But I must say, I felt bad for Clio."

Cookie frowned. "Felt bad for her? Why?"

"She was quite upset," Maris said and described the constant dabbing of the eyes, and even the sobbing.

"I don't understand," Cookie said, and fetched the pot's lid. She turned down the flame under the soup and covered it. "Because of the murder?"

"She hinted at that," Maris agreed, "and being interviewed by Mac."

Cookie opened the oven door and checked the bread. "Then I imagine that's it." She closed the oven and turned to Maris. "She can't possibly be upset about Langston Spaulding himself. Not after what I heard the other day."

Maris looked at her, surprised. "You heard something the other day? Here?" Cookie nodded as she fetched some cheddar from the refrigerator. "Why didn't you say something?"

Cookie put the cheese on a cutting board, and shrugged. "One hates to speak ill of the dead."

"One does," Maris agreed. "One would

also like to have as much information as possible."

The diminutive chef, grimaced a little, but stopped what she was doing. "I heard him berating Jayde, actually shouting at her as they came downstairs."

"Shouting at Jayde?"

"Something about putting their clothes away in the dresser. He obviously had been looking for a dress shirt he couldn't find."

"And he yelled at her about that?"

"I couldn't believe it," Cookie said. "But the worst part was the way that she kept apologizing for making him angry." Cookie shook her head. "I don't know how she put up with him." But after she fetched the cheese cutter, she paused. "You want to hear my theory about people like Langston Spaulding?"

Maris nodded, unwrapping the aged cheddar. "Please," she said.

"Only super nice folks can stand to be around people who are so rude and self-centered," she declared. "All the normal people have fled. People like Langston Spaulding count on that."

As Maris put the cheese on the board and picked up the cutter, she thought back on some of the more unsavory guests she'd dealt with in her hospitality career. From loud and obnoxious to demanding and belittling, it was hard to remember their companions. They'd simply been part of the background. Maybe Cookie was right. Maris regarded the chef. That wasn't too surprising.

Cookie got a small spoon and went to the stove. She lifted the lid on the soup and sampled a bit. She nodded as she turned off the flame, then smiled at Maris. "I'd say that's done. Shall we have some?"

22

Though Mikhail had not been tempted by grilled cheese sandwiches and tomato soup—apparently Russian comfort food was borscht with a dollop of sour cream—Maris had thoroughly enjoyed both. Once they'd cleaned up, Cookie had decided to use the B&B's typical afternoon lull to work in the herb garden. But back in her room, Maris was nagged by a different task. She glanced to the top of the armoire where Glenda's pretty silk brocade boudoir box sat, but she didn't need to bring it down. Inside, she knew exactly what she'd find. More importantly, though, she knew exactly what was missing.

As a child, Maris had always admired and wanted to wear a particularly pretty pendant that Glenda had kept there. But later her aunt had told her that the faceted green stone wasn't a necklace at all, but a pendulum. But when Maris had opened the box where it had always been kept, it was empty. Over time she'd searched every inch of the room, looking in every pants' pocket and even moving furniture, but to no avail.

With a sigh, she stared at the big metal skeleton key hanging on the hook next to the door, then stood up straighter, strode to the key, and took it. In the utility room, she shut the door behind her and looked down at the large, black metal lock in the floor. Below it was the basement.

"Basement," she muttered to herself. "Not elevator."

It'd probably been unavoidable that, in her many stays at many hotels with many problems, she'd eventually run across a malfunctioning elevator. Though the manager had later assured her that her life had never really been in danger, it certainly hadn't felt like that. The few hours that she'd spent trapped in total darkness and without communication had seemed dangerous in the extreme. Though it'd been years and thousands of miles ago, she hadn't forgot it. Her photographic memory had seen to that.

She gripped the key tightly in her sweaty hand, turned it in the heavy metal mechanism, and heard the familiar scrape and clunk of the metal tumblers. Once the key turned freely, she pulled the big wooden hatch open. The stairs below descended into darkness.

Rather than stare down into it, she quickly laid the hatch to the side, went down a few steps, and flicked on the light switch. The long fluorescent bulbs below hummed and tinked for a few seconds and then blinked to life.

"That's better," she said, exhaling. The light always made it more tolerable.

As she sat on the steps, she closed her eyes and took a deep and calming breath.

"It's just a basement," she whispered, and felt for the hatch door. "The door is open."

When she opened her eyes, she looked down the stairs. "You're fine," she told herself, and moved down to sit on the next step. "You're fine."

But the words didn't stop the rising tide of anxiety that had started in the pit of her stomach. As she gazed at the steps and the brick floor below, her chest started to tighten. Quickly, she looked to the bookcase that paralleled the stairs. Instantly she felt a little calmer, and reached out to touch the lustrous leather spines with their gold lettering. Aunt Glenda must have amassed the small library recently, since Maris didn't remember it from her youth. As she gazed at the various volumes, a question occurred to her, and she picked up the book titled *Magick Folk*. She turned to the index in the back.

Presto.

It was the word she'd heard Aurora say twice when she'd sold the grill. She found an entry immediately and turned to the page. It seemed that presto, like abracadabra, was part of a broader category called magic words. They were used with a few different types of magical abilities, including one to control the weak-minded. A suggestion, followed by the magic word, could trigger the weak-minded to obey it.

Maris thought back to Aurora and the couple buying the grill. That had to be it. They'd initially balked at the price but quickly changed their minds. She smiled a little to herself. That type of magical ability must come in quite handy in the retail business. But as she recalled the altercation with Langston Spaulding, her smile faded. Could Aurora have used the power of controlling the weak-minded to somehow kill him?

She put the book back in its place and steeled herself for another attempt to descend. Again, she scooted down a step, such that her shoulders were level with the utility room floor. Then, before she could overthink it, she went down yet another stair, still sitting. Determined to make at least a little progress, she gripped the edges of the hatch opening. Then, with a deep breath, she ducked her head low and peered into the basement, her eyes just below the level of its ceiling.

The basement was huge. Not only were there more bookcases filled with books and piles of magazines, there were also a couple of antique trunks, some wooden crates, and cardboard boxes. Beyond the bookcase there was an old chest of drawers that looked like an antique. On top of it was a battered old leather suitcase, complete with faded stickers. On top of the suitcase sat what looked like a carved wooden duck. If Maris wasn't mistaken, there was a pile of hat boxes as well. She frowned a little. As far as she could recall, Aunt Glenda hadn't worn hats.

A light scratching from the utility room door made her jerk upright.

"Gads," she exclaimed, gasping and putting a hand over her thumping heart.

Then a plaintive, harmonica-like meow came from the door, followed by more scratching.

"*Mojo*," she breathed.

With relief, she got up from the steps and opened the door. But rather than come inside, as he had in the past, he simply looked up at her with his big orange eyes, gave his signature meow again, and trotted off across her room.

"Really?" she said, a bit exasperated. "You're not even going to come in?"

He stopped at her open bedroom door, looked over his shoulder at her, and meowed again. Then he disappeared into the hallway. Now she had to frown. What in the world was he up to? But then she checked her watch.

Of course. It was his dinnertime.

Back on the stairs to the basement, she turned off the light, then closed the hatch and locked it. As she went back into her room and hung the skeleton key she smiled a little. At least she'd made a bit of progress.

23

As Maris headed to the kitchen, she passed the parlor and had to stop. Mojo was sitting on the floor in the midst of a spilled box of tarot cards.

When she'd first returned to Pixie Point Bay, she had admonished the little black cat for making this kind of mess. But now she knew better. His skill with the Ouija board was matched by his talent for the tarot. As she watched, he got to his feet and sauntered among the scattered cards, some face up and others face down. But at one in particular, he stopped. Gingerly, he picked it up in his mouth—and began to chew.

Before he could really gnaw on it, Maris quickly scooped him up.

"No," she said quietly and took the card in

her fingers. "This is not dinner. Let me have it." But his big eyes only seemed to get bigger as he stared at her. "Let it go," she insisted, and tugged on it. "Come on, Mojo. Let it go." He began to squirm, and she gave him a stern look. "I'm not putting you down with this card in your mouth." She looked into his eyes. "Period."

Suddenly he stopped his squirming and his jaw dropped open. Maris quickly took the card and looked at it.

"The three of swords," she said, and shuddered a little at the image. Against a background of clouds and rain, three long, gray swords pierced a big red heart that hovered in the air. "Good grief," she muttered.

There was no doubt that Mojo had once again chosen an apt card, but it shed no new light on Langston Spaulding's murder. Yes, the man had been stabbed through the right atrium, but not three times.

"*Mojo*," Cookie called from the kitchen. "*Salmon.*"

Executing a near back flip, Mojo jumped from her arms.

"Be careful," she said, though she needn't

have, as he landed lightly on his feet. He sped from the room, galloping toward the kitchen.

As she picked up the rest of the cards, she kept the three of swords on top of the deck, pondering it. She gently tapped her temple, brought up a memory of the interpretation booklet, and read the card's meaning. When dealt in a spread, the three of swords represented unhappiness, heartache, and sorrow. Maris frowned at it.

Again, that all applied to Langston's death, but wouldn't it to anyone's?

With a little sigh, she put the cards back in the box and replaced them on the bookshelf. It had to mean more than that but, as usual, she'd likely have to wait to find out.

24

───────

In the kitchen, Maris was pleasantly surprised to discover Jayde sitting at the butcher block and having some of Cookie's tomato soup. "Jayde, I'm so glad to see you eating."

The slim woman wiped her mouth with a napkin, and smiled. "I could hardly resist. The smell upstairs was just divine." She glanced at the near empty bowl. "And the actual flavor was even better."

"There's plenty more," Cookie said from the counter. "How about another bowl?"

Jayde shook her head and held her tummy. "I am positively full, but thank you. It was wonderful."

Outside the kitchen's window, the sky was growing dusky as evening approached.

Though it was a tad on the early side for the Wine Down, Maris decided to get started with the setup, hoping it might encourage Jayde to eat a little more.

As Maris went to the fridge for the cheese, Jayde asked, "How old is Mojo?" She was watching the pudgy black cat contentedly eating his smoked salmon in the corner.

"Our best guess," Cookie said, "is about five years. He was a rescue."

"A rescue," Jayde said, putting her elbow on the large wood block and resting her chin in her hand. "It's hard to imagine anyone not wanting such a pretty cat."

Maris smiled at her as she set down the cheeses on the block. "I couldn't agree more." She fetched the cheeseboard from a shelf. When Jayde made to get up, Maris held up a hand. "You're perfectly fine there," she said. "There's plenty of room." The slim woman sat back down.

Though Maris would have typically put together the Wine Down in the dining room to encourage conversation and a relaxed atmosphere, she decided she already had that in the kitchen and started to slice the cheese. As she prepared the different varieties, she chatted with Jayde about the dairy in Cheeseman Village and how much she'd enjoyed the factory tour.

"This cheese is local?" she asked, taking an interest in it for the first time.

Maris nodded, speared a slice of parmesan and offered it to her. "It's as local and fresh as it could possibly be." She watched as Jayde took the slice and gave it a tiny bite.

"Mmm," she said. "Very tasty." But Maris noted that she didn't immediately eat the rest.

"Tonight I'll be pairing it with our local wine," Maris said. "So it'll be an 'all local' wine and cheese tonight."

"Really?" Jayde said, with more interest. "You have local wineries?"

"Cheese from up north," Maris replied, "and wine from down south." She picked up the nearly finished cheeseboard. "Here," she said, "I'll show you."

As Maris had hoped, Jayde followed her into the dining room. After she set down the cheeseboard, she turned to the wine cabinet, removed a Merlot and opened it. She poured a bit into two of the waiting wine glasses, and offered one to Jayde.

"The Alegra winery has been winning awards almost since their first release," Maris said. She lifted her wine glass to Jayde. "Cheers."

Jayde clinked her glass and then took a sip. "Oh, that's smooth," she said, and took another little bite from the parmesan she'd brought. "Oh, yes, that's a perfect combination."

Maris smiled. "I'm glad you think so." She set down her glass. "I'm just going to get a few more things from the pantry. Be right back."

By the time she returned with the nuts, dried fruits, and chilled Chenin Blanc, Jayde had poured herself a full glass of the Merlot. Maris heard the front door open, and the Schellings quickly appeared at the dining room entry, looking a bit bedraggled. As Maris opened the Chenin Blanc, she said, "Long day out?"

Mia set her backpack on the floor next to the wall, and Andrin did the same. "Hundreds of photos," she said, "and not a single one does it justice." She nodded to Jayde and went to pour herself a glass of the white wine. "I'm giving up."

As Maris arranged the fruits and nuts, Andrin took a plate and began serving himself. "It's uncanny," he said, and popped a dried apricot in his mouth. "It's as though the light is somehow different." Mia handed him the wine. "I don't understand it." He took a long swig.

As Maris poured more wine for herself, and then Jayde, she said, "I assume you're talking about the lighthouse?"

"The most beautiful lighthouse," Mia said, taking some Gorgonzola from her husband's plate.

Maris turned to Jayde. "The Schellings are lighthouse enthusiasts. They travel the world visiting them."

"Is that right?" Jayde said.

As they fell into conversation about their travels, Maris saw that the Merlot was almost empty and opened another. She'd just set the cork aside when Mikhail appeared.

"I hope I am not too late," he said, smiling at them all, his book tucked under his arm.

"Of course not," Maris said, returning his

smile. "And there's more where this came from. Please, help yourself."

"Try the Merlot and the parmesan together," Jayde said, but she slightly slurred the last word.

Mikhail eyed her as he moved to the sideboard. "Good together?" he asked her.

"The best," she said, waving her glass and spilling a little wine, although she didn't notice. Mikhail, though, had. He brought the bottle to her and filled her glass. "Thank you," she said, grinning, and Maris saw the flush in her cheeks and the slightly glassy look to her eyes.

In the course of twenty-five years of Wine Downs, Maris had seen it all—including one young man who'd gotten so drunk that he actually slipped right under a table. She was attuned to all the warning signs and used any number of means to avert disaster: suggesting that they eat more food, or drink more water, or perhaps take a glass to their room. But in Jayde's case, she did none of these things. The last thing she'd suggest to the poor woman was being alone. Nor did she have any intention of stopping her from drinking. Newly widowed, if she wanted to get drunk, then she could get drunk. But Maris was relieved when Jayde took a seat.

"The Schellings were just telling us about photographing the lighthouse," Maris said to Mikhail.

"What kind of camera are you using?" Mikhail asked.

"Cameras plural," Andrin corrected, as he fetched more cheese. "I prefer the square medium format, while Mia prefers the 35mm."

His wife smiled at him. "It's just his way of delaying the composition choice. Eventually he crops them rectangular."

"True," he said, pouring some wine. "But also I shoot with film. Mia is all digital."

"We have yet to develop the film, of course," Mia said, "but the results with the digital were disappointing—particularly for a digital artist."

As the Schellings told Mikhail of their woes, trying to photograph the lighthouse from a boat they'd chartered, Jayde interjected, a touch too loud, "Isn't it harder from a boat?"

"I think it is," Andrin said. He tossed a hand in the air. "But the view was incredible."

"Well," Jayde said, trying to get to her feet. "Maybe you should–"

Her supporting hand slipped on the table, and when she made a grab for her chair, she inadvertently tossed her wine glass, which crashed on the floor.

"Oh no," Mia said.

Mikhail immediately went to Jayde and helped her sit back down.

Maris hurried to the sideboard and grabbed a handful of napkins and a small wastebasket. Luckily, the glass had been empty. She quickly picked up the shards, and dropped them into the bin.

"I'm so sorry," Jayde said, swaying in her seat. "It was an accident."

"Of course it was," Mikhail said to her, keeping her upright.

Maris set aside the waste can and quickly stepped over to Jayde. She took her firmly by the elbow. "Let's see if we can manage the stairs." Mikhail took the other arm and together they got Jayde to her feet. Maris put her arm around the woman's waist. "I think we can manage," she said to the art dealer. "Come on, Jayde," she said, taking her from the room. "You're going to be fine."

25

If Jayde hadn't been so slim, Maris wouldn't have managed it. But step by slow step, she was able to support and guide her, and pull them up using the handrail.

"I'm drunk," Jayde said, clinging to her as they reached the middle landing.

Maris turned them to face the second short set of steps. "Yep," she said, starting the final climb. "I think that's safe to say."

Jayde whipped her head around to look at her, causing them to sway. "You're a good person."

Despite the situation, Maris had to laugh. "We'll see what you think in the morning." She pulled them up the last few steps. "Last one. Here we go."

"*Up*," Jayde said, as though she were part of a circus act.

With no small amount of relief, Maris steered them to her room, and through the door. As though the goal was in sight, Jayde lurched forward picking up speed. Maris barely kept her from colliding with the bed, turning her so that she could sit, instead of fall.

"I win," she announced, bouncing a bit.

Maris took a moment to catch her breath, but smiled at the tipsy woman, who was grinning. "Yes, you do," she said, and thought, *we both do*.

"Let's see about these shoes," Maris said crouching down, but a firm hand clamped down on her shoulder. For a moment, Maris thought the woman meant to stand, but Jayde was simply staring at her.

"Do you wanna know a secret?" she said, still slurring. She checked over Maris's head, and then from side to side.

Though Maris was pretty sure that she didn't want to know a secret, it wasn't going to be easy to stop her. "Everyone loves a secret," she said, noncommittally.

"Boy, do they," Jayde agreed, with an exaggerated nod. "But this one's a doozy." She leaned forward and Maris had to hold her up so she didn't topple. "My husband," she whispered harshly, "and Mikhail." She glanced at the door. "Were in cahoots." Then she pushed Maris away and leaned back to see her reaction.

Maris's brows drew together, as she bent to take off one of Jayde's shoes. "Cahoots?"

"Don't play dumb," the woman said, almost shouting. "Cahoots! You know. They did deals together."

Maris tugged off the other shoe. "What kind of deals?"

Jayde sighed and rolled her eyes. "Art deals, of course." She began to sway. "Forgeries." Her eyes began to close. "They sold forgeries."

As Jayde flopped backward, Maris lifted her ankles and managed to get her legs on the bed. "They sold..." Maris began, but Jayde had completely passed out, her eyes closed and her mouth open.

Gently, Maris folded the comforter over her legs and hips, turned off the lamp on the nightstand, and quietly closed the door behind her. But as she came down the stairs, she frowned. Mikhail and Langston Spaulding sold forgeries? Together? Mikhail had certainly made a good show of disliking the art critic, if Jayde was right. Although Maris would like to question Galkin about it, she couldn't imagine he'd admit it.

Only when she reached the dining room did she realize how quiet the house had been. The room was vacant, the backpacks gone, and the empty glasses were on the sideboard. Apparently Jayde's departure had signaled the end of the evening.

A plaintive and tinny little meow drew her attention to the floor under the dining table. Maris looked underneath. "Mojo," she said, as he came trotting over. "Thanks for waiting for me." Her fingers gently ruffled the soft hair behind his ears. "Let's get this cleaned up."

She took the cheeseboard and its few leftovers to the kitchen, and then returned for the wine glasses, with Mojo close on her heels. Though she loaded the glasses into the dishwasher, she washed the board by hand and left it in the drying rack. Back in the dining room, she wiped down the sideboard, the table, and the wine cabinet, all the while thinking about what Jayde had said. As she folded the rag up, she suddenly remembered her flash of precognition at the side of the house, and also what Claribel had showed her.

"The nurse paining," she said to Mojo, as she bent to scoop him up. He purred as she took him to her room, where she tossed the rag in the hamper. As she closed her bedroom door, she determined to have a look at the painting herself.

26

Before Maris had managed to get to the kitchen and help Cookie with breakfast, her cell phone rang. Mojo lifted his head and glared at it on the night stand. Maris petted his head as she picked up the phone and checked the Caller ID.

As she smiled, she accepted the call and said, "Good morning, Jude."

"Good morning, Maris," he said, in his bass voice. "I know I'm not calling too early."

She laughed a little. "Not when you own a small business." Mojo's head sank back to the comforter. "What can I do for you?"

"Actually," he said, "I've got a couple things for you. First, I have a buyer for Glenda's truck, and I've also found a car that I think you might like."

"So soon," Maris said. "That's fabulous. Should I stop by the shop?" Though she'd intended to head over to Inklings, the gas station was on the way.

"If you have time, that'd be perfect."

"Works great for me. I'll be right over," she said. "See you soon."

When she hung up, she stepped into her shoes and looked at Mojo. "You hold down the blanket fort while I'm gone, okay?" His only answer was a stretch of his front legs before he completely relaxed again. "Good," she said and grabbed her purse.

At Flour Power, Maris pulled in and parked next to the sub shop. Though she was tempted to go in and get a cup of Fab's coffee, she saw that the big door to the garage was open. As she'd expected, Glenda's blue truck was there but, to her surprise, so was Jill Maxwell, looking into its bed.

"Jill," Maris said. "Good morning. What a nice surprise to find you here."

"Surprise?" the nurse practitioner said looking up at her. "I'm your buyer."

Jude came around from the back of a car parked next to the truck. "I didn't know you knew each other."

Maris stared at the two of them. "Jill wants to buy Glenda's old truck?" She looked at the big vehicle. "What in heaven's name for?"

"Saddles," Jill said. She pointed into the bed. "A couple of hay bales will fit there. The saddles there. Shovel. Tack. Boots." She grinned at the two of them. "It's ideal."

Maris came over to the bed to look inside, half expecting to already see it filled. Instead it was empty, and very clean. "You ride horses?" Dressed in her blue scrubs and white clinician's coat, she didn't at all look the part.

Jill moved around to the back of the truck. "I ride dressage." Maris followed her to the back. "Competition riding all over the area." She pointed to the bumper where a shiny new metal ball gleamed. "I'll finally be able to tow my own trailer."

"Jill is giving up her car too," Jude said. "I think you might want to take a look."

Maris turned to him. "Really? Where is it?"

He smiled. "You're standing right next to it."

Maris almost jumped as she whirled around. "This car looks new," she exclaimed. "Why would you give it up?"

"It's not new, but thanks," the nurse said.

"I bought it before I started riding. It's just not right for me any more."

"But it is low mileage," Jude said. "Here, let me give you a tour." He started at the back, lifting up the hatchback. "The full width hatchback is nice for shopping."

Maris nodded. "Which I do quite a bit of, for the B&B." He pointed to the front wheels. "All wheel drive, for the windy coast roads." They moved around to the front of the car and he indicated two yellow looking head-lights alongside the regular ones. "Fog lights," he said, then popped the hood.

Maris held up a hand. "Stop. You've sold me."

Jude gave her a pained look. "But I haven't gotten to the good part yet."

"It's all good," Maris assured him, and he closed the hood. "What are you asking?" she said to Jill.

The nurse was sitting on the passenger side of the truck's bench seat. "I was going to ask you the same thing."

Jude stepped between the car and the truck. "I've taken the liberty of looking up the value of both vehicles," he said, easily able to reach a hand to each roof. "I'd say it's pretty even."

"A trade then?" Jill asked, getting out.

"If you're both amenable," he said.

Maris grinned at them. "You have got yourself a deal." She stuck out her hand and Jill grasped it.

"Deal," the nurse said as they shook on it.

"I'll go get the paperwork," Jude said and headed to the sandwich shop.

They both watched him go. "He's amazing," Jill said, just as Maris said, "Wasn't that nice." They both laughed, each of them turning to their new vehicles.

"Oh," Jill said, "I've been meaning to ask how Jayde is coping."

Maris thought of last night's drinking episode, and how hungover the poor woman would be this morning, but decided to skip that part.

She sighed a little. "I'm afraid she's having a hard time of it, although I think that's to be expected."

Jill nodded. "Grief can be so different for different people." She paused and put her hands in the pockets of the white coat. "I wonder if a sedative or an anxiety med might help." Then she shook her head. "Oh, but what am I saying? Jill can take care of that herself."

Maris's brows drew together. "Take care of it herself? How?"

"Jayde used to be a nurse, before she met her husband. We talked about it at the exhibit."

Maris recalled the two of them near the "Pedigreed Nurse." "Is that why you were both looking at that painting?"

Jayde laughed a little. "That weird thing. Yes, I think we were bizarrely drawn to it." She paused for a bit. "Honestly, I think we bonded over it."

Maris remembered how kind Jill had been to sit with Jayde after the murder, and had given her a ride to the coroner and then home. She glanced out the garage door. Now more than ever, she was sure she needed to see that painting.

When Jude returned with the paperwork, Jill signed first. "I'd love to stick around and chat, but I've got to go open the clinic." Jude handed her the keys to the truck and she grinned madly. "Thank you both. This has really made my day—week and month."

As Maris and Jude watched, she hopped in the truck, started it up, and drove off with a couple of honks and a wave.

"That truck purred like a kitten," Maris said, looking after it. Then she regarded Jude. "Nice job."

"I gave both vehicles a tune-up, a few new belts, an oil and filter change, and a good clean."

Maris stared at him. "You are the one-stop shop. But you can't run your business by doing car swaps without taking a cut. I insist. You must let me pay for the repairs and all the maintenance work."

Jude shook his head. "It's the least I can do. If not for your aunt's loan to us, we wouldn't be in business."

"Fine," Maris said. "Then consider it paid."

Jude's eyes widened. "I'm afraid I couldn't do that. The two amounts aren't even comparable."

Maris made a show of taking her phone from her back pocket. "If you don't take a digital payment method, I'll go get my checkbook."

"There's no charge," he insisted.

"I'm afraid there has to be," Maris insisted back. "Are you running a business or not?"

He cast a glance at the door to the sandwich shop, and then at Maris's new car. "All right, how about this?" Maris crossed her arms over her chest and waited. "I'll throw in...ten oil changes and tune-ups."

Maris thought about it and did a quick calculation in her head. She stuck out her hand. "You've got yourself a deal."

His big hand engulfed hers and they shook. "Thank you," he said. "And Glenda."

She smiled up at him. "It's just good business." Then she glanced at the car. "I'm going to have to pick this up later, if that's okay."

"Sure," he said. "It'll be right here, but are you sure you don't want it for shopping?"

She shook her head. "I'm not going shopping today, I'm going picture hunting."

28

Maris parked directly in front of the bookstore and hurried inside. She found Minako on the first floor standing next to an open box of books, stacking them on the shelves.

"Minako," Maris said, breathing a bit hard. "There you are."

"Good morning, Maris," Minako said smiling, until she took a good look at her. "Are you all right?"

"I'm fine, just in a bit of a hurry."

Minako set the books down. "In a hurry? For a book?"

Maris smiled a little. "No. Sorry. Not a book. I'd like to see a painting from the exhibit. I assume they're still here?"

Minako inclined her head. "They are, but they have already been packed away."

"Ah," Maris said, her shoulders sagging a bit. She was too late. It'd be highly unlikely that someone would uncrate an exceedingly expensive painting just because she asked.

But Minako must have seen her disappointment. "Is there a problem?"

Maris could hardly say that her magical lighthouse suspected that something was wrong with the painting or that a drunk Jayde Spaulding had confessed that her husband and Mikhail Galkin sold forgeries.

"It's just that I'd hoped to see the nurse painting before it was shipped," she said.

"Oh, the one by Damien Previs," Minako said. Her face brightened. "I have something almost as good. Let me show you."

The shopkeeper led Maris to the artwork section, where the books were arranged in order of the artist's name. Large, glossy coffee table books filled the shelves. Minako went directly to the 'P' section and selected a particularly large volume.

"*Damien Previs, A Retrospective*," she said, taking it to a nearby sitting area and placing it on the table. "It has every known work of his, both privately and publicly held."

"Oh really?" Maris said, suddenly interested. "How lucky for me."

"I wouldn't exactly say lucky," Minako said, opening the book to its index. "We made sure to have at least one book for each of the artists who were exhibited."

Maris smiled at her. "Of course. How business savvy of you."

Minako flipped through the pages to a certain section. "All of the nurse paintings are grouped together, as are his other series."

As the shopkeeper turned the book so that Maris could see it, she discreetly tapped her temple. An image from the exhibit immediately popped into her mind. But when she reviewed the nurse section of the book, all paintings in the same pulp novel style, she found fourteen: "Timely Nurse," "Serengeti Nurse," "Royal Nurse," and eleven more. Yet none were titled "Pedigreed Nurse" or had exactly the same image.

Maris cocked her head at the paintings, turned a page to the next section, and a page back to the previous section, but there were only fourteen. "You're sure these are all of his works?"

In answer, Minako turned to the introduction, by Damien Previs. She scanned down the first paragraph with her index finger. When it stopped, she read, "the first ever collection of all my works." She looked up at Maris. "I have to assume that is true."

If it was, Maris thought, then "Pedigreed Nurse" was a forgery.

"I know it's boxed up," she said, "but can you take me to it anyway?"

"Of course," she said, "it's out on the loading dock."

Maris followed Minako out to the back where they found Alfred using a manual forklift to move a pallet of book boxes. More importantly though, an armed uniformed guard was also there, bringing Maris up short. But as she looked around at the wooden crates, she immediately understood. There might be a small fortune in artwork here, and it couldn't be locked up, nor would it fit in the store.

"Maris, hello," Alfred said. "I'd ask what brings you to the dock, but I suspect–"

"It's the Damien Previs nurse painting," Minako said.

Alfred's eyebrows rose, and the security guard turned his head toward them. "Oh, well as you can see, all of the paintings were crated–"

"Right after the exhibit," Minako said, "to protect them from damage."

"Of course," Maris said, eyeing the guard.

Claribel had shown her the painting for a reason, and Maris had assumed that she should therefore see it. And yet that seemed like it was impossible.

Playing for time, she said, "Do you know which crate it's in?"

"That's easy," Alfred said, stepping to the small mountain of wooden boxes.

Minako pointed. "It's the one in the back, the big one."

The guard finally stepped forward. "I'm afraid I can't let anyone move the artwork," he said.

For a moment Maris considered invoking the murder investigation. But in reality, she knew that only a search warrant could compel anyone to do anything.

She smiled and nodded to the guard. "I understand," she said simply. "Thank you."

Alfred and Minako exchanged a look, then he shrugged. "I guess I'll bring in the rest of the books."

As he went back to the forklift and lifted the pallet he'd slid it under, Maris said, "I'm sorry for troubling you two. Clearly you have plenty to do." She'd just been about to turn away, when Alfred pulled the pallet toward him and something glinted on the floor where it had just been.

Minako spotted it as well. "What is that?"

Alfred stopped. "What is what?"

But just as Minako bent down to pick it up, Maris said, "Stop!"

Everyone on the dock froze, except for the guard whose hand went to the pistol on his belt.

"Minako," Maris said, as calmly as she could, "don't touch that." The diminutive woman took a step back. "Do you have a paper towel, or a plastic bag, or maybe some tissue?"

She nodded and hurried back inside the store, as Maris stepped closer to take a look.

"What is it?" Alfred asked, just behind her.

Maris crouched down, staring at the finds. "A lipstick and an eyeliner." Minako came running back from the store, and showed Maris a tissue, a paper towel, and a plastic bag. "Perfect." Using the tissue, she picked up the lipstick without touching it and put it in the bag. Then she used the paper towel and did the same with the eyeliner. She held up the bag and they all gazed at the contents.

"I think I'd better call Mac," she said.

29

In the living room of the B&B, Maris surveyed the strange assembly of people. Jayde and Mikhail sat together on one side of the room, while Aurora and Clio sat together on the other. Mac stood near the door, and Maris stood opposite him in front of the fireplace. As usual, Aurora was easily the most flamboyant of the attendees, in vivid red robes with a matching head wrap and makeup. She was also the most impatient.

"Aurora has a business to run," she said to Maris. "She would appreciate your being quick."

Maris nodded to her. "I intend to do just that." She gazed around at the group. "Thank you all for coming."

"Was there a choice?" Clio asked, glaring at Mac. Maris noted that her eyes were still puffy and red.

The sheriff calmly looked at her. "Yes, and you could leave now, if you like." He hooked his thumbs in his utility belt. "But I'd recommend you stay, for your own good."

"Gods," she muttered, glaring at the floor as she put a tissue to her nose.

Aurora patted her shoulder. "You will be fine." Then she pointedly looked at Maris.

"Only one person here had an altercation with Langston Spaulding," Maris told her.

Aurora sat up straighter and leveled a steady gaze at her. "Aurora begs to differ. She had two."

"According to descriptions from every quarter," Maris said, "including your own, you two were at odds. You were at the gala that night, and according to the estimated time of death, you could have been on the loading dock when Langston Spaulding was killed."

"All true," the shopkeeper replied. Her bright eyes darted around the room. "Also true for everyone here."

Maris turned to Clio. "Of course, the painting knife only implicates one person here."

Clio's lips pressed into a thin line as she banged her fists on her legs. "How many times do I have to say this? I'm a watercolorist. I don't use a paint knife. That's for thick paints like oil or acrylic!"

Maris shook her head. "You mostly paint with watercolor. It's certainly what you're known for. But if your studio was searched right now, are you saying you don't even own one?"

Clio glanced from side to side. "I don't know!" she nearly wailed. "I might have one, and even a canvas." Aurora patted her shoulder again. "I don't know," she said, hunching a bit and looking at the floor. "I have no idea."

"I don't doubt you," Maris said. "I also don't doubt that you were never at odds with Langston. In fact, if I had to guess..." Maris looked at Mikhail and then back to Clio. "...I would imagine that the social media sparring between you two was arranged." She gazed at Mikhail. "How many times have I heard that even bad publicity is still publicity?" Then Maris looked at Clio, who averted her gaze. "Enough times to understand that your public dislike of Langston was an act." Though Maris waited, neither Mikhail nor Clio said anything—including denying it.

Maris turned to Jayde. "I'm glad to see you're feeling better, particularly after last night."

Though Mikhail stiffened, Jayde only smiled. "I apologize for getting drunk, and thank you for helping me to my room."

Maris smiled back. "In fact, I'd say your recovery is nothing short of remarkable. Without the slightest trace of a hangover."

Jayde's smile faltered for a brief second and a wary look stole quickly across her face. "I took some aspirin and made sure to hydrate myself. Thank you."

Maris shook her head. "You're not hungover, because you weren't actually drunk."

"Really, Maris, what is your point?" Mikhail asked. He gestured around the room. "Why put her through all this? We all saw that she was drunk. Why bring it up now?"

"Because she had a little secret to tell me about you, while she was supposedly drunk."

Mikhail scowled at her. "Nonsense," he said, but he sounded less sure of himself. "I have no secrets."

"Or perhaps none that Jayde should have known about," Maris said, looking into his eyes. "But you and Langston were working together."

Mikhail scoffed. "I despised the man," he declared.

"Like Clio," Maris pointed out. "But unlike her, you and Langston were selling forgeries."

The art dealer's head cocked back as though he'd been slapped. "What? This is preposterous." He stood. "I thought we were here about the murder."

Mac took a step into the room. "We are, Mr. Galkin. If you'll please have a seat, you'll have your turn." When Galkin wavered, Mac said, "Please sit down."

Maris looked at Jayde again, her expression supremely composed. "While it may be true that your husband and Mikhail sold forgeries, your bit of news about it was your second attempt to deflect suspicion." Jayde only raised her eyebrows in response. "Your first was using the painting knife to cast suspicion on Clio." Maris glanced at the artist. "When in fact Clio is the last person who wanted to kill Langston, since she was having an affair with him."

Aurora grimaced and stared at the young woman, who only buried her face in her hands and quietly cried.

"Shut up," Jayde told her. "Just shut up. I knew about the affair. I've known about all of them."

Clio raised her head and stared at the woman. "What? What do you mean all of them?"

Jayde snorted. "You don't seriously think you were the only one," she sneered. "You're the fifth."

"At first," Mac said, "the puncture of your husband's heart seemed a rather unlucky stroke. His death was instantaneous, and no chance for a rescue. But with some medical knowledge, someone might be able to tell exactly where to place the tip and easily push in the thin piece of metal."

Maris noted a sudden twitch in Jayde's eye. "Jill Maxwell told me that you and she talked about your former profession: nursing."

Mikhail turned to stare at her, and inched away.

"Do you recall that evening in the ladies room?" Maris continued. "Aurora and I were in front of the mirror."

"She rushed in," Aurora said, recalling it. "She was going to put on lipstick."

"But when you checked your purse," Maris said, "you realized you didn't have any and left."

Jayde's eye twitched, but she met Maris's gaze. "I said not a word to either of you, and you've fabricated this entire scenario about what I did or didn't want to do."

The sheriff held up an evidence bag. "Not exactly." Everyone stared at the lipstick and eyeliner, including Jayde.

"Did you drop your purse on the loading dock?" Maris asked. "I imagine it'd be hard not to, while stabbing someone."

Clio gasped and covered her mouth with both hands. Aurora crossed her arms and stared at Jayde. Mikhail whipped his head around to look at her.

Though Jayde opened her mouth as though she might say something, she closed it.

Mac lowered the bag. "I called in a favor," he glanced at Maris. "Maybe a couple for the rush test. The DNA from the makeup, the DNA from the blade of the paint knife, and the DNA from your broken wine glass all match." He strode toward her, setting the bag down on the coffee table. He removed the handcuffs from his belt and stopped in the middle of the room. "Jayde Spaulding, I'm placing you under arrest for the murder of your husband."

Still not uttering a sound, she stood and put her hands behind her back.

"You can have a seat, Mrs. Spaulding," the sheriff told her. "These aren't for you." He looked at Mikhail, who'd gone pale. "We've been in touch with artist, Damien Previs. Not only does he not know you, there is no painting called 'Pedigreed Nurse'." He motioned for Galkin to stand. As he did, Mac turned him, drew his hands behind his back, and put on the cuffs. "Mikhail Galkin, I'm arresting you for fraud and transportation of stolen goods." He nodded to Jayde. "The following applies to you both." He recited their rights to them as Maris, Aurora, and a horrified Clio looked on. When he was done, he said, "Let's go."

He picked up the evidence bag as he motioned for a docile Jayde to precede him and an apparently shell-shocked Mikhail. But before they left the room, Mac glanced over his shoulder. "Nice work," he said to Maris.

She felt some heat rise to her cheeks, but smiled and said, "Thanks."

Clio buried her face in her hands again. "I can't believe it," she said.

Aurora stood and placed a hand on the artist's shoulder. "Do you need a ride home?"

Clio took in a deep breath and raised her head. "No, I've got a class to teach." She gazed up at the shopkeeper. "But thank you." She checked her watch. "In fact, I'm going to be late." She stood and picked up her purse, but paused and looked at Maris. "I don't know how you figured it out, but I'm glad you did." Without waiting for a reply, she turned and hurried away.

Aurora watched her go, and shook her head. "Aurora thought the young lady had better taste." Then she shrugged. "Still one doesn't judge the artist, just the art. Aurora is disappointed but will continue to carry her work." She regarded Maris for a moment. "Next time you're in Magical Finds, stop by for tea."

Maris smiled at her. "I'll do that."

In the late afternoon, Maris sat on the back porch with her watercolors, paper and jars of water. Taking a page from Clio Hearst's book, she decided that if you wanted a lovely painting, it couldn't hurt to start with something lovely. Although Maris had never realized it before, the quality of light at the ocean was different. Maybe it was the moisture in the air, or perhaps the salt, but since she had started looking at scenes with an eye toward painting, she'd noticed that the light at the seaside was softer and more glowing.

Of course, capturing that on paper was a different matter.

But rather than worry about it, Maris practiced what they'd learned in their first class: loose and flowing movements without striving for perfection. Footsteps just inside the house exited onto the porch, and Maris looked up to see the Schellings. They wore their backpacks and had their suitcases. Andrin carried a large thin paper-wrapped parcel under his arm.

"How perfect," he said, looking at what Maris was doing. "We visited the gift store in town yesterday and bought a painting of your lighthouse." He hefted the parcel under his arm. "Ten times better than any photo we took."

"We just wanted to thank you for your hospitality," Mia said. "We had a wonderful trip."

Maris smiled up at them. "I'm so glad," she said. "It was fun for me to learn of your hobby, and I hope you'll come back for another visit."

Mia nodded. "That will be our goal."

"After we see the rest of the lighthouses on our list," Andrin said, but then he looked up at the Old Girl and smiled at his wife. "Maybe."

The pleasant young couple bid Maris their goodbyes and left, with just a couple more glances at Claribel. As Maris resumed painting, she remembered her remote viewing. Had the Old Girl been trying to tell her that the murderer was a nurse? And Mojo's tarot card. Had the three swords represented Aurora, Mikhail and Jayde—the three people who had despised him?

Another, softer set of footsteps drew Maris's attention to the porch door. With a steaming mug in each hand, Cookie exited. Maris left her brush in one of the water jars, and accepted the mug.

"Thank you, Cookie." She inhaled the aroma. It was chamomile, likely from the chef's own herb garden, with a dollop of honey. She blew on it and took a sip. "Mmm. Perfection."

"That's really nice," Cookie said, indicating the painting with her cup. "You've got a talent for this."

Maris chuckled. The Old Girl's conical tower was crooked, the ocean behind it leaked into her windows, and the horizon was bowed.

"I see you've left your reading glasses inside," Maris said.

Cookie grinned at her. "Oh I don't mean

that painting." She squeezed Maris's shoulder as she turned to go. "I meant the relaxing."

Maris had to laugh out loud. But as she gazed out toward the bay and the ocean beyond, she wondered if Cookie might not be right.

Another Pixie Point Bay book awaits you in The Witch Who Knew the Game (Pixie Point Bay Book 4).

For a sneak peek, turn the page.

The Witch Who Knew the Game

Excerpt

CHAPTER ONE

Maris Seaver couldn't remember the last time that dinner had been served at the Bed and Breakfast. But as she sat at the dining room table with Cookie and the B&B's four guests, she had to wonder if it wouldn't be a fun thing to do. Of course, since Cookie didn't regularly prepare lunch or dinner, it'd have to be done as it was being done tonight.

"For our first course," Etienne Fournier said, bringing the small white plate to Maris's place mat, "a salmon canapé."

The owner of Plateau 7, the five-star restaurant on the bay, was dressed in the traditional chef's uniform and hat. In his early sixties, he was of medium height with dark hair and flinty black eyes, and a pointed mustache that was waxed to a precise perfection.

"Local salmon on a fresh cucumber slice," he continued, setting the next plate in front of Cookie. "Finished with a lemon truffle mayonnaise."

The French chef finished by serving the big man at the head of the table, Reggie Atkinson. A red-head with a matching red beard and hazel eyes, Reggie was the leader of the group. He'd reserved the entire B&B for the weekend and arranged for the catered dinner months ago. He called the get-together a company off-site for the key employees of his business: Whiz Kids Games.

"Bon appétit," the chef bid them.

Reggie smiled down at the little morsel, and then at each member of his group. "Let's start."

"This looks amazing," Pammy said, reaching for it. But when the Filipino man next to her picked up his fork, she paused. Then she picked up hers.

Blonde, blue-eyed, and more than a touch on the nerdy side with her round, black glasses, Maris had already noted that she and Felix were pals. He waited for her to spear the appetizer and then they tasted it together. Her eyes widened as she made an appreciative sound, and nodded.

Her neighbor's dark eyes lit up as he enjoyed the canapé as well. Like Pammy, Felix was in his early thirties. But unlike her or the rest of the group, he was easily the least nerdy, with his artsy goatee.

"I like this," he said, bringing a napkin to his mouth. "A lot." He reached for his glass of white wine.

Reggie had used his big fingers and simply popped the cucumber and salmon in his mouth. He nodded, still chewing. "Very nice," he said around the food. "What do you think, BJ?"

The final member of the group had used a knife to cut his in half and had finished the first section. He'd just been about to eat the second piece, but paused. "I'm savoring it," he said with an enormous smile. "I'd eat this all evening if I could."

BJ sat on Reggie's left hand, and was even

more nerdy than Pammy. Probably in his mid-forties, his dark hair had gone prematurely gray and he wore it very short. But it was his enormous fluorescent green glasses that marked him as the nerdiest. Or perhaps it was avant garde. Maris couldn't decide.

What she did know, however, was that the canapé was divine. The brined salmon melted in her mouth, and the cucumber had a fresh and crisp texture to compliment it. The lemon truffle mayo left a nice lingering aftertaste that did indeed leave her wanting more.

Cookie nodded. "Perfect," was all she said.

The French chef inclined his head toward her, his mustache lifting at the sides, but said he nothing. He glanced around the table, and began to remove the plates.

Maris turned to Reggie, who was finishing a sip of wine. "Are you planning on seeing some of Pixie Point Bay's local sites while you're here?"

"Oh, absolutely," the big man said, his equally big voice rumbling. "It's finally a chance for us all to unwind a bit."

"I'm looking forward to seeing the redwoods for the first time," BJ said, his smile lifting his bright green glasses.

"I'm going to do something out on the bay," Pammy said, watching the chef set down a bowl in front of her. "Oh, this looks *wonderful.*"

"French onion soup," he said. "Sweet onions in vegetable stock and white wine, seasoned with garlic, thyme, and pepper." He set the next bowl down in front of Felix. "Topped with Gruyere and Swiss cheese, of course." He went back to the tray on the sideboard.

"Felix," Maris said to him, "are you planning to get out?"

He laughed a little as he picked up his spoon. "I don't remember what that's like."

"Oh my god, is that the sun?" Pammy joked as she pretended to squint.

"Look, the sky," BJ chimed in. "It's still blue."

As Maris was served her soup, she smiled up at the chef, before he proceeded to Cookie. She looked around the table. "I take it you all work long hours?"

There was laughter again, just as the last soup was served to Reggie, who said, "That smells amazing." Without a moment of hesitation, he dug in.

Maris tasted a bit of the broth, and her appreciative "Mmm" joined the others. For a few minutes, there was only the sound of happy diners. A seemingly simple dish, the soup struck just the right balance of the savory onion with the salty and creamy cheese.

"I've changed my mind," BJ announced. "Now I want *this* for the rest of the evening."

Everyone chuckled a little, too busy eating to make more jokes.

But eventually Reggie answered Maris's question. "We put in some crazy long hours," he said, "and this is a well-deserved getaway."

"Thank you, again, Reggie," Pammy said.

Next to her, Felix nodded. "Yes, thank you." Pammy elbowed him and indicated his goatee. He took his napkin from his lap and quickly wiped it. She nodded.

Conversation turned to the lighthouse, and Maris filled them in on its Victorian heritage, the conical white tower being built first, in 1885. Then the lightkeeper's house, today's

B&B, following a few years after that. But as Etienne cleared away the soup bowls, Maris was curious about what the group did.

"I take it that Whiz Kid Games makes games?" she said.

"So to speak," Reggie said. "Actually, we're a publisher."

She cocked her head at him, but before she could ask him what a game publisher did, Etienne reappeared with the main course: crab legs, enormous ones. Appreciative murmurs and a low whistle went up from around the table.

"Fresh caught Dungeness crab," he said, putting the first of the three plates he carried in front of Reggie, "with cheesy potato pancakes and steamed carrots." He set the next in front of BJ. "With local organic greens topped with an aged balsamic vinaigrette." He set the third plate in front of Pammy and headed back to the kitchen.

Cookie had been taking a sip of water, but when she set it down, she turned to Reggie. "So you publish games, not create them."

Reggie had been staring at his plate, but looked up at her with a broad smile. "We do a bit of both." He glanced at the sideboard, to a small stack of pamphlets that Maris hadn't noticed. "In fact," he said, as he got up and brought them back to the table, "it's easier to demonstrate than explain."

Maris noted that the other diners had gone still, and were glaring at the pamphlets. The French chef returned with the four remaining plates and served them, in total silence. Although everyone had their dinner, no one moved to eat.

"You have got to be kidding," BJ said, glaring at Reggie as his hand clenched the stem of his wine glass.

Reggie ignored him and focused on Cookie. "You'll be fascinated to know that our upcoming publication is a murder mystery dinner." He handed two pamphlets to Cookie, and she passed one to Maris. He arched his eyebrows at Maris. "And it just happens to take place at a Victorian B&B."

"No," Pammy muttered and sat back, while Felix moaned and put his head in his hands, as he said, "I should have known."

Maris exchanged an alarmed looked with Cookie. The convivial five course meal had just devolved into something else.

Reggie opened his pamphlet. "Shall we?"

• • • • •

Buy The Witch Who Knew the Game

FREE BOOK

If you'd like to learn how Maris arrived in Pixie Point Bay and got her start, you can read *The Witch Who Saw the Light* for FREE by signing up for my newsletter at the link below.

Get A Free Book

DEDICATION

For Mr. Bee's Knees

COPYRIGHT

Copyright © 2020 Emma Belmont

tion of this book via the Internet or via any other means without the permission of the copyright owner is illegal. Please purchase only authorized electronic editions, and do not participate in or encourage electronic piracy of copyrighted materials. Your support of the author's rights is appreciated.